AOLÉON

The Martian Girl

PART TWO

**This is Part Two of a five-part series.
Parts one through five are:**

Aoléon The Martian Girl – Part 1: First Contact

Aoléon The Martian Girl – Part 2: The Luminess of Mars

Aoléon The Martian Girl – Part 3: The Hollow Moon

Aoléon The Martian Girl – Part 4: Illegal Aliens

Aoléon The Martian Girl – Part 5: The Great Pyramid of Cydonia

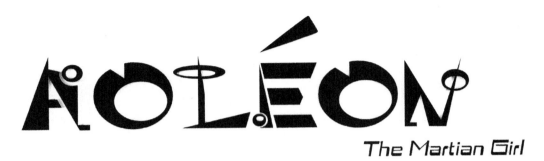

AOLÉON

The Martian Girl

PART TWO

Brent LeVasseur

For all media inquiries, publishing, merchandising, or licensing:
aoleon@aoleonthemartiangirl.com

For information regarding permissions, e-mail Aoléon USA at:
aoleon@aoleonthemartiangirl.com
or use the Contact Us page at:
http://aoleonthemartiangirl.com

Visit Aoléon The Martian Girl website for more information at:
http://aoleonthemartiangirl.com.

ISBN Hardcover: 978-0-9791285-4-7
ISBN Paperback: 978-0-9791285-3-0
ISBN eBook: 978-0-9791285-0-9

Published in the U.S.A.

Welcome to Part 2 of a five-part series.

TABLE OF CONTENTS

LUMINESS

CHAPTER SIX

Whoohooo*!*" Gilbert cheered as he ran and jumped high into the air using the newly found power of his suit combined with the slightly lessened gravity of Mars relative to the Earth. He had almost superhuman strength and speed.

"Please, you must not draw attention to yourself," Aoléon cautioned.

"Oh, sorry. I'm having so much fun, I can't help it," Gilbert said smiling guiltily at her. "It's just that I can't do that on Earth. I feel like Superman in this thing. It's fantastic!"

"Superman?"

"You know — he's a superhero from the planet Krypton that can fly."

"Ahh," Aoléon said in recognition as if she had just snatched the image of Superman right out of Gilbert's head the moment he thought about it.

"You reading my mind again?"

Aoléon shrugged. "Blue tights and a red cape," she giggled.

They emerged from a side artery lined with giant spherical buildings and headed onto a main thoroughfare and toward the city center.

"What is that huge building there?" inquired Gilbert as he gazed toward the city center where a gigantic citadel stood perched above all other buildings in the far distance.

"That is the Luminon's palace," replied Aoléon.

Buildings stretched out in front of them as far as Gilbert's eyes could see, and saucers flew back and forth overhead, swarming like insects. Just above them, a giant Martian ship hovered, projecting an enormous holokronic broadcast of yet another public service announcement from the Luminon to the crowd of Martians below.

An advertisement for a Martian rock band called Andromeda Supernova and the Black Holes appeared. The closest thing Gilbert could think of to describe it was a neon day-glow, head-banging, Martian, punk rock band complete with a Zero-G mosh pit. They were scheduled to play at the Galactic Stadium after a very successful sold-out gig at the seedy underground club, Emo's Paradise.

As they moved further along the street, Gilbert could hear the band's music playing in his head like a bad pop song that wouldn't go away. Amazingly, the music was not being broadcast over loudspeakers but was somehow being beamed directly into his brain, bypassing his ears completely.

Man, if the governments back on Earth got hold of this technology, they could beam whatever thoughts they wished us to think directly into our brains, thought Gilbert who tried unsuccessfully to block the music playing in his head.

Aoléon smiled and nodded. "For all must agree with all, and they cannot know if their thoughts are the thoughts of all, and so they fear to speak. And they are glad when the candles are blown for the night," recited Aoléon bringing Gilbert out of his thoughts.

"Huh?" wondered Gilbert. "I don't get it."

"*Anthem* — by the Terran author, Ayn Rand," replied Aoléon.

"You read our books?"

"I have not exactly read them myself, but *someone* sure did. I just remembered it!" Aoléon exclaimed laughing. "Which is exactly my point — being telepathic, my thoughts and memories are not always my own. Your individuality in spirit, in thought, and in your wide range of emotions is what makes Terrans unique among all other races of sentient beings. In a sense, I think many other races either envy or fear you — for what you are and what you might become."

"Really? I had no idea."

"Really," Aoléon said, smiling.

"And what might we become?" wondered Gilbert.

"That is a question only you can answer."

"You're incredibly wise for a teenage Martian girl."

"Well, I am considered to be a teenager by other Martians, primarily because the average life span of a Martian is more than 1,000 of your Terran solar years. As a fifth-density being, we live outside of your third density, linear time. So we do not age like you do, and we do not keep track of time like you do. However, by your calendar, I am approximately 108 years old."

"One hundred eight years old! Oh — my — gosh, you're older than my grandmother!"

"Yes, but on Mars I am just barely beyond childhood age. We achieve our 'age of awakening,' which is similar to your 'puberty' around the age of 20 Terran solar years."

"So you must think I am some kind of baby then."

"No, of course not, silly. You are cute, though," said Aoléon, winking at him. Gilbert blushed. "If you do not believe me, share my thoughts."

"I believe you," Gilbert said, reddening further under his blue makeup.

Pockets of paladin guards stationed at the sides of the street stood in formation with their strange, black-and-emerald-green-hued armor glinting in the Martian sunlight. The paladin armor resembled a robotic exoskeleton that apparently enhanced the Martian wearer's strength, agility

and speed. The armor augmented the physical stature of the Martians who wore it and made them appear more physically intimidating.

"The Luminon's Royal Paladin Elite Guards," whispered Aoléon, motioning toward the formation of Martian shock troops goose-stepping in formation.

As they walked through the crowd, Gilbert noticed that Martians were lining up along the sides of the street like salamanders in the sun and were being ushered aside by more Royal Paladin Elite Guards. Aoléon and Gilbert had stopped to discover what the commotion was about when they saw a large procession heading down the street toward them. Gilbert watched the paladin guards marching in rows, followed by a hovering chariot.

"It must be the Luminess," Aoléon explained.

"The Luminess?"

"The spouse of the Luminon and matriarch — our leader."

Gilbert saw that inside the hovering chariot stood a tall, slender Martian woman wearing an ornate body suit and headdress. The Luminess's eyes shone silvery grey, and her expression was dour. Ice prickled Gilbert's spine as her gaze locked on his. The corner of her mouth twitched slightly with a glint of recognition. In that moment, Gilbert could sense her reaching into his thoughts and he into hers.

For a brief moment, Gilbert saw the Luminess for who she really was — all of her history, her insecurities, her flaws, and her deepest, darkest secrets flew through his mind in flashes.

Her face wavered slightly as if it had been a television signal that suddenly was interrupted. Her head and face seemed to shape-shift into a completely different form — a form that quite closely resembled a *lizard*.

Gilbert shuddered as he quickly looked away, but it was too late. The Luminess raised an arm, and the procession came to an abrupt halt. With her eyes fixed on Gilbert, she beckoned him telepathically.

Come here boy! commanded the Luminess with her mind. Her mouth did not move, and no sound came out. It was as if Gilbert's mind were somehow being coerced into obedience. On the surface, he felt compelled to do her bidding, but deep down his senses were screaming danger! His instincts took over, and he used every ounce

of his mental might to resist the temptation to obey. The Luminess scowled, sensing his resistance. A white flash of light enveloped him, and suddenly he was back in his bedroom at home lying in his bed.

After a few moments, his heart rate slowed, and his fear of danger quickly subsided. He exhaled deeply and told himself to relax. Glancing over his shoulder, he saw his kitty, Xena, lying atop his dresser and intently watching Gilbert. After a moment, she got up, scampered over to him, and curled up on his chest. Xena lay there and started to purr while Gilbert stroked her soft fur. As he relaxed in the comfort of his own bedroom, Gilbert began to forget about what was happening and told himself that it had all been just a bad dream.

Suddenly, Xena started to talk. It sounded as if she were speaking to him, but it also sounded just like the purring noises she normally made when she was content. The purring voice was gently commanding him, calling out to him, and beckoning him to come closer.

Although Gilbert thought this was a bit strange at first, he still felt comfortable being there with Xena. She was about the most comforting thing he had in his life, yet deep down in his subconscious, he sensed that something was terribly wrong.

Am I dreaming? I never heard Xena talk before, not even in one of my dreams. And she is commanding me. This is very strange. Gilbert then listened more closely to his cat speak.

"Prrrr…come to me!" Xena said in a barely understandable voice. Although Gilbert was in a dreamlike state, he seemed to realize at some level of his consciousness that it wasn't a dream. At that moment, his stomach sank, and his instincts once again took over. Thoughts flooded through his mind as he realized that it was the Luminess who was projecting a false holographic vision of his cat into his mind!

"You're not Xena!" blurted Gilbert's dreamlike self angrily. Suddenly, his bedroom transformed into a murky tunnel, and Xena transmuted into a dark, demonic noncorporeal being. He could not make out the face of the creature, only the dark amorphous shape of its body and its eyes, which he could clearly see glaring at him, burning like stars in the darkness.

Sensing evil, Gilbert quickly prayed for strength. He felt a surge of power like a lightning bolt shooting down his spine. His whole body became illuminated. Cornered, Gilbert charged. For a moment, he actually sensed fear in the demon as light emanating from his charging body defeated the darkness. With his hands outstretched, concentrated beams of light shot from them and struck the horrific form, destroying it in a burst of light. In that instant, Gilbert quickly returned to consciousness. It took him a couple of seconds to realize that he was back with Aoléon on Mars. He felt mentally drained as if he had suddenly awoken from a deep sleep.

"Quick! Run!" Aoléon cried out. Grabbing Gilbert by the hand, she pulled him back through the crowd, away from the Luminess and her paladin guards. Gilbert stumbled and ran as fast as he could, knocking over several Martians while his Martian spacesuit greatly augmented his speed and strength.

Seize them! commanded the Luminess, using her telepathic link to the paladin guards as she collapsed, unconscious. The guards turned and chased Gilbert and

Aoléon through the crowd. They came to a dead end and, just as the paladin guards were about to come around the corner, Aoléon grabbed Gilbert and waved her hand in a small circle around her waist. They began to walk up the side of a building.

"How…how is this possible?" Gilbert gasped as he gazed down at the street below.

"Shhhh! Not now," Aoléon snapped.

Aoléon and Gilbert moved up the side of the building, around its perimeter, and down the other side. They ran down a side street and made a series of turns to put as much distance as possible between them and their pursuers.

"That was close!" Aoléon exclaimed as she waved her hand over her waist, thus disabling the gravity displacement device that had enabled them to walk up walls. As they turned another corner, they pushed their way through the dense crowd and headed down another street that led to a small village.

"What happened back there?" inquired Aoléon.

"The Luminess. She looked at me, and the next thing I remember, she was trying to control my mind. She called me to her! And–and–s-she impersonated my cat!"

"Although we have the ability of mind control, we seldom use it on others. It is forbidden. This is very strange indeed," Aoléon responded with a forlorn expression.

"There's more."

"What?"

"For an instant, I thought — I thought I saw the Luminess transform into a *lizard*."

"A lizard?"

"Yeah, it was freaky."

"Would you share your thoughts so that I may see what you saw?"

"You have to ask? I thought you did that constantly."

Aoléon closed her eyes briefly in concentration. "Ahh… I see what you mean. This is very disturbing indeed. I think that we should do what Pax asked us to do and investigate this further. Hopefully, we can find out what is really going on."

"How?"

"We will try to sneak into the Luminon's Palace and see if we can discover anything out of the ordinary."

"Isn't that dangerous?"

"Ummm, affirmative. We could die."

"Oh. Is that all? By all means let's do it then," Gilbert smirked.

"Sarcasm is something we are not accustomed to here. It is refreshing, as is your sense of humor. Few Martians have one. Now come inside to meet my family," Aoléon said, relieved to be only a short distance from the safety of her house.

Aoléon's home was a slightly dilapidated structure not unlike a blue metallic mushroom joined to a spherical base. The primary difference between her house and the others nearby were several stone objects situated around the front yard.

"Those are my father's sculptures," said Aoléon. "Each one is carved from an ancient stone taken from various ruins on the surface of Mars. Each contains a history. The ancient peoples of Mars imbued their memories upon them. Each one tells its own unique story."

"How does it tell a story?"

"Let me show you," said Aoléon as she took Gilbert's hand and touched it to one of the sculptures. The instant his hand made contact with the surface of the stone, imagery began to flash through his mind. He saw pictures of an ancient civilization on the surface of Mars. The Martians were living above ground during a time when there was a thriving ecosystem and when oceans adorned the planet. He saw something else that startled him...*humans.*

"Absoludicrous! Wait! Were those *humans* I saw?"

"Yes. Your ancient ancestors originated from the constellation *Lyrae.* Before they were brought to Earth, they lived here on the surface of Mars. But that was a very long time ago. Come on. We need to go inside. We are already late for evening consumption, and I fear my mother is growing anxious."

The duo entered to find Aoléon's mother sitting behind a table that hovered in the center of a curved room. She stood up to greet them. Gilbert noticed that she was relatively short like Aoléon, just barely under five feet tall, had a soft round face, two large blue eyes, and a slender nose that complemented the shape of her face. Dinner was being dispensed from tentacle tubing that extended from the ceiling above the table, filling bowls with a milky substance.

"We have postponed daily consumption to await your arrival, but your father and I are growing hungry. Who is your guest?" Phobos, Aoléon's mother, motioned to Gilbert who stood nervously in the entryway. Then she gasped as she realized that Aoléon had brought a Terran home for dinner. The two quickly exchanged conversation telepathically. Gilbert, however, was not privy to that conversation — only to their changing facial expressions that indicated some kind of conflict between them. The brief communication ended with Phobos saying, "Aoléon! How could you?!"

"We had no choice. We were chased, and if I had not taken Gilbert with me, there is a good chance he would have been nullified by the hostile farmer." Aoléon hesitantly smiled at her mother. "Please amplify your calm, mother… let me introduce you to my new friend. He is a Terran who will be staying with us for a few days. If that is permissible with you and father, of course."

"Welcome to our home. Please make yourself comfortable," Phobos said to Gilbert while gracefully gesturing with her elongated arm and blue three-fingered hand.

"Thank you, mother," Aoléon said with a bit of relief in her voice. "Gilbert, this is my mother, Phobos."

"Nice to meet you, ma'am."

"Are you hungry? You must be famished after that long journey."

"Sure am. Uh, what exactly do you eat?"

"Mainly galact. It is similar to your cow's milk with additive enzyme emulsion for digestive ease," replied Phobos.

"You don't happen to have anything other than Martian food, do you?" Gilbert let his words slip out without thinking, and Aoléon's family just stared at him for several moments without responding. "On second thought, thanks anyway!" Gilbert said with a blush as he removed the candy bar he had stowed in his pocket. He realized the second after he had spoken that he might have offended them by turning down their offer for food.

"Mother, may I order a platter since we have a guest?" Aoléon asked a bit tentatively.

"Yes. You may," Phobos replied.

"Platter?"

"It is similar to your pizza."

"You eat pizza?!" replied Gilbert, shocked.

"Yes, of course. No civilized world can exist without it, silly. Here on Mars, we make it with galact. Would you like some?" asked Aoléon, beaming.

"Sure would! As long as it doesn't come in a tube…just kidding," he said. "Um…actually, I'm serious."

"I know. I can read your mind, remember?" She winked at him.

"Oh, yeah, I forgot," Gilbert laughed.

"Great. Galact platter it is, then!" Aoléon said as she skipped off across the room toward the holokron.

Gilbert placed his candy bar back in the pocket of his spacesuit, exhaling with relief.

"Galact platter please," said Aoléon to the holokron. After a moment, a cycloptic Martian appeared on the screen ready to take her order. "I would like to order two extra-large galact space platters with extra asteroids on top — for delivery. You know my coordinates. Fine." She walked away from the holokron, and it returned to broadcasting regular Martian programming.

"Asteroids?"

"Basically spicy galact in solid form, similar to your sausage or meatball, but it is not meat. I once tasted one of those on Terra at a restaurant called 'Pizzaiolo' in a place your people call 'Oakland.' Unfortunately, I could not digest it because it was meat."

"You're not vegan are you?" Gilbert asked.

"Vegan? Oh, of course not! Vegans live in another solar system in the Lyra constellation. My people originated from the Andromeda constellation." Aoléon waved her arms, and a holographic star map appeared, except that it wasn't a map. It looked exactly like a three-dimensional view of Andromeda. Gilbert had seen them through his small telescope many times, but this was much different. The colors in the nearby Andromeda Galaxy shone vividly with crimson reds, dark purples, and green gaseous vapors. For the first time, he could see it from all sides by moving around it in three dimensions.

"Uh, no I meant a vegetarian," Gilbert chortled. "You see, on my planet when people don't eat meat and eat only vegetables, they are called 'vegans,'" Gilbert said.

"Oh! I see!" Aoléon said, laughing as the holographic image vanished. "Yes, I cannot eat meat."

"Hold on…you said you're from Andromeda? I thought you were from Mars?"

"Well, yes. I was born on Mars. However, Mars is just a settlement colony, not our true home world. Long ago, our people originated from the constellation Andromeda and came to this solar system to settle on Mars."

"Oh," Gilbert cleared his throat.

"The reason why I have cyan-colored skin is because the ancient Andromedan home world orbits around a binary star system where the larger star, Alpheratz A, is a bluish spectral B-type subgiant star with an unusually high amount of mercury, manganese, and certain other metals in its photosphere. It is the special nature of our star that caused us to evolve with bluish-hued skin. Had our people originated here in the Sol System, we would probably have skin similar to yours."

"I didn't know that."

"Also, we have blue, copper-based blood, but your blood is based on iron and is red."

"Um, is that like your phone and your TV?" Gilbert asked, pointing at the holokron.

"Yes, sort of. We all can communicate telepathically, but sometimes things get a bit mixed up, so we still use the holokron."

"Oh yeah? What kinds of shows do you have? My mom doesn't let me watch TV that much. Only after I've finished my chores and my homework and, even then, most of the time I'm not allowed. She says watching TV makes your brain go fuzzy."

"Well, besides the Luminon's channel, we have about a thousand others. There are how-to shows such as *The Tinkerer's Guide to Saucer Maintenance*. Cooking shows such as *The Joys of Galact Cooking*. And sports — my favorite is *Pro Psi-ball*."

"You sure love your galact. Being on a farm around cows all day, shows about milking cows or making cheese are about the last thing I want to see when I watch TV."

"Well, we have a lot to do. Come, let me introduce you to my father."

Aoléon walked through the house to a room in the back where her father, Deimos, sat hunched over a block of metal. Gilbert watched him making cuts while bits of molten metal fell to the floor. He looked closer and noticed that Deimos wasn't using any device to make the cuts but was wielding a crystal that seemed to magnify his psionic powers into a concentrated plasma beam. The beam sliced through the dense block of metal like a knife through gelatin.

While Gilbert stood watching Deimos, a small animal hopped over, sniffed him, and rubbed up against his legs. It was a three-eyed, furry blob with large rolls of skin that resembled a cross between a longhaired cat and a pug. Aoléon explained that it was her sister Una's pet. Gilbert tentatively stroked the alien animal. He could hardly believe that it could move, given its bulbous shape, short stubby legs, and tiny paws.

Then from the other room, Aoléon's pet moog, Zoot, rushed over to him, looking for attention. Zoot was a furry critter with a chubby body and head that sprouted two protruding antennae that curved upward to attach to two tennis-ball-sized eyeballs. Zoot also had a large mouth shaped like a funnel and a tongue that could shoot out and grab things at a great distance like a bullfrog catching a fly. Zoot fought for Gilbert's attention. Despite his strange appearance, Gilbert thought Zoot was fairly cute. Zoot noticed the other animal and took off chasing it around the room and creating havoc. Gilbert quickly picked up his feet to avoid colliding with the two animals as they dashed around the room.

As Aoléon watched the commotion, a bemused smile spread over her face. Using telepathic suggestion, she commanded the two animals to leave the room. They resentfully obeyed, sulking as they scurried away. She turned to Deimos who ignored the ruckus; his attention was focused on making precise cuts into his metal sculpture with his psi-crystalline plasma torch.

"Greetings, Father."

Deimos looked up and smiled at Aoléon. "Greetings, Aoléon." He deactivated the torch and lay down the crystal. Deimos was tall with broad shoulders, a round protruding nose, large mouth, and small blue eyes. He wore a utility suit that could be his work clothes thought Gilbert.

"How was work today?" inquired Aoléon.

"Production has slowed. It would seem that many of the bovars in the Galactworks have gone missing. And how are you, my child?"

"Well…I was practicing for my pilot's test. I took the saucer for a ride around the galaxy and visited Terra. Permit me to introduce you to my new friend, Gilbert. He will be staying with us for a few days." As she spoke, Zoot came back into the room and started to rub against Gilbert's legs.

"Hello, sir," said Gilbert as he tried to keep Zoot away from his legs. He clumsily hopped around a bit on one leg until Aoléon came over, picked up the thing and put it in another room.

"Hello, Gilbert! Welcome!" said Deimos. *Aoléon, you brought a Terran here…to our home?* Deimos spoke via a private telepathic link with Aoléon. Gilbert could tell they were communicating because both Deimos's and Aoléon's facial expressions suddenly changed.

"I had no choice, Father. We were being chased by another larger Terran and his three-legged pet. He intended us harm, so we both fled together. Then we were chased by a… oh well, never mind. I promise I will take him home in a couple of days," Aoléon replied, wringing her hands.

"You must be extra careful. He should leave as soon as you are able to take him back," spoke Deimos firmly.

"Yes, Father."

"I also think it is a good idea for you to stay away from Terra for a while."

"I understand, Father."

Aoléon and Gilbert walked into the main living quarters where a holokron situated in the center of the room was showing large bulbous Martian animals, which Gilbert surmised were the Martian versions of Earth's milk-giving cows. Machines then processed the milk into *galact*.

"Does that mean I'm stuck wearing this blue makeup?" Gilbert exaggerated a pout, sticking out his blue lips while crunching up his eyebrows.

"Unless you would like to be turned into galact, I suggest you do so…for both our sakes."

"Really?"

Aoléon winked at him. "Very cute," she replied, giggling. Gilbert turned pink beneath his blue makeup, giving his face a purple glow.

BIZWAT THE PROCYON

CHAPTER SEVEN

LOWER FEEB DISTRICT ENCLAVE
MARTIAN MEGALOPOLIS
OLYMPUS MONS
PLANET MARS

Bizwat was a Procyon — part of an elite order of Martian special forces soldiers, a hallowed warrior in the highly secretive Martian Military Intelligence Service. As a Procyon, he had the esprit of an honored war veteran and the swagger of a martial arts expert — at least an alien one. But even that wouldn't do Bizwat justice because he had powers and technology that would make most elite soldiers drool with envy.

The kit the Procyon possesses does not compare to his well-honed skills — for as any Procyon would tell you, it's the man (or in this case, the Martian), not the gear, that makes a Procyon best in class.

As a Procyon, Bizwat carried a special-purpose pulsed-plasma rifle. But in close quarters combat situations, Bizwat

preferred his pair of psi-plasma blades. Crystals embedded into the arms of his Procyon body armor amplified Bizwat's psionic power to form a coherent beam of plasma hot enough to cut through any solid object.

All Procyon are given a secret identity (a cover). In the home world of Mars, Bizwat was a Saturn Pizza delivery person who swore a solemn oath to accomplish his mission of delivering every pizza within 30 cycles or less, or the meal would be free.

Bizwat cut through the dense Martian air traffic like a plasma blade slicing through a space slug. He piloted his velocipod via telepathic link as if it were an extension of himself. The velocipod resembled a motorcycle that had been turned upwards on its front wheel. It had a dome over the front that created an enclosure around his entire body; two small, but powerful, gravity displacement propulsion engines; and a pair of 360-degree rotating disruptor cannons attached to the bottom in case a delivery went really bad. On Mars, pizza delivery was a serious business, and the Procyon didn't mess around.

Bizwat arrived at Saturn Pizza Headquarters and flew into the obligatory delivery chute, a tube tunnel that passed

completely through the Saturn Pizza Headquarters building allowing all Procyon to load their cargo without having to leave their velocipods. The delivery hatch opened in the rear of the velocipod, and a storage rack extended outward, anticipating the loading process even before coming to a complete stop. Packbots, tiny, orb-like robots with small arms and pincers, immediately emerged from a delivery hatch near the rear of the pod carrying a platter storage container.

The packbots performed a mechanical aerial ballet, flying over and around each other while loading the platters into the cargo compartment of the velocipod. After completing the loading process, they quickly departed the way they came. As the Procyon hit the button to close the hatch, the first delivery coordinates transferred immediately to the velocipod's navicomputer. Bizwat accelerated out of the chute toward his first destination: Aoléon's house.

The velocipod was built for speed and agility. In the hands of an experienced operator such as Bizwat, the velocipod could easily maneuver through the dense air traffic over the Martian megalopolis, of which there was plenty this night. Clusters of burbpods, larger transportpods, and even larger cargopods became the main obstacles. Bizwat maneuvered around them like a slalom ski racer sweeping from side to side as he advanced toward the finish line.

Bizwat arrived at Aoléon's house with plenty of time to spare. He exited his pod, removed Aoléon's platters from the delivery hatch and walked up to the entrance. Inside the house, an alarm rang, and Aoléon appeared at the door almost immediately. They both stared at each other for an instant as Bizwat stood there in his Procyon uniform holding her platters.

"Oh! Bizzie, is that you?" Aoléon beamed.

Bizwat's Procyon helmet retracted into the neck of his suit, revealing a youthful, handsome Martian face. "Great to see you, Aoléon. Here you go: two extra-large platters with extra asteroids on top."

"Thanks! Can you spare a few cycles to come inside? I have someone I would like you to meet."

"I can remain for a brief interval, and then I must depart. I have another delivery to make after this one."

"I would like you to meet my new friend, Gilbert, a Terran."

"A Terran, huh? Are you making crop circles again?" he chortled, grinning like a cat that had just trapped a mouse in its claws. "You know what kind of trouble you would be in if the Xiocrom ever found out you had a Terran here…eh?" Bizwat said, raising a blue, hairless eyebrow at her. Aoléon exaggerated her pouting lips, thrust her arms down to her sides, and quickly arched her back, making her appear almost as tall as Bizwat.

"No one is going to find out," she said, waving her arm toward Gilbert. "Bizwat, meet Gilbert. Gilbert, this is Bizwat, a friend of mine. Do not let his appearance fool you. He is a bit of a genius with a nanocom, and Mars' greatest plasma sword fighter. No one can hack an A.I. construct or duel better than he can." Bizwat turned slightly bluer in the cheeks than usual. "And I never thought I could make a commando blush," Aoléon teased.

"It's an honor to meet you, sir," said Gilbert.

"You, too. Do not believe everything she says. I gave up hacking and sword fighting long ago. Now I just deliver platters. What part of Terra are you from?"

"I am from a state called Nebraska, which is part of the United States in North America."

"Ah yes. I have heard of that place. It is farm country, no? Lots of milk cows there, right?"

"Yes. Among other things."

"Our organization has recently taken a special interest in your planet — probably because you have so many cows."

"Why would Martians be interested in our cows?"

"We need milk. We need it for things such as platters, galact and, of course, my favorite: chocolate galact ice cream!"

"Haa! I can't believe it! You eat ice cream, too?"

"Yes, but we mostly eat galact. Healthy, but it tastes like it sounds — bloody awful! On Mars, galact production is big business. If the galact stopped flowing, we would have riots and unrest."

"But why do you need our cows? Don't you have your own?"

"Until recently, we did. We call them bovars. They are not like Terran cows, of course, mainly because they are not mammals in the traditional Terran sense. They have no hair, for example, and are hatched from large eggs. But they do produce a milk-like substance that is similar in nutrient and enzyme composition to your cow's milk. A couple of weeks ago, they all but disappeared. We are not sure what happened to them — it is currently under investigation. Galact production has ceased," said Bizwat. "It is all a strange mystery."

"That's horrible!" replied Aoléon.

"So you're going to take our cows?"

"That is a possibility, even though it goes against our prime directive — a strict nonintervention policy — mainly because it seems the Luminon is pushing for war," said Bizwat, looking perplexed. "Which is most odd because the Luminon has always stood for peace," Bizwat said, raising an eyebrow.

"We encountered Pax on the way home," said Aoléon.

"Did you report him?"

"Negative, but he asked us to spy on the Luminon to find out what is going on," Aoléon continued.

"How do you expect to do that?" a worried expression crept over Bizwat's face.

"We were going to try to sneak into the Luminon's Palace." Aoléon revealed a wry smile. She could sense Bizwat's thoughts before he spoke.

"Gilbert, Aoléon tends to act against her better judgment."

Gilbert chuckled, nodding in agreement and thinking back to his experience with her making crop circles and being chased by the United States Air Force.

Aoléon grinned at Bizwat. "At least I will be remembered for something."

Bizwat turned toward Aoléon half smiling. "You already know my thoughts. So I will not say be careful, but there it is anyway," Bizwat guffawed. "In the meantime, I will make some unofficial inquiries to see what else I can dig up," he added, nodding toward Gilbert. "Nice to meet you, Gilbert. Now I have to levitate. Aoléon, stay safe and do not do anything *too* stupid."

"Thank you for the vote of confidence," Aoléon retorted, "And you," she nodded slightly, tilting her head sideways while moving her arm in an outward Fibonacci spiral from her heart in the traditional Martian greeting of love and peaceful tidings.

Bizwat gave them an off-hand salute, climbed into his velocipod, and shot off into the night. Aoléon and Gilbert went back into the house to sample their pizza.

⊚⊚⊚

AOLÉON'S HOUSE, MARTIAN MEGALOPOLIS, OLYMPUS MONS PLANET MARS

The family gathered around the dining room table (a hovering holographic elliptical disc transformed into a tabletop and floating in the middle of the room). Gilbert found it almost impossible to sit because each of the five "chairs" resembled an oversized exercise ball. Except instead of it being made of inflated rubber, it consisted of a holokronic force field projection. But still, Gilbert found it almost impossible to stay balanced on the ball and eat at the same time. He kept sliding from one side to the other. Aoléon, meanwhile, sat perfectly perched cross-legged in Buddha-like fashion on top of her ball with her hands folded neatly on her lap.

At first attempt, Gilbert sat down on the chair too quickly and immediately fell over backwards. Blushing, he picked himself up off the floor, rolled the ball back into position near the table and tried it again. This time, he sat down slowly and made a concerted effort to stay balanced. Gilbert smiled at Aoléon, proud that he had finally situated himself without falling.

"Haha! I got it!" he exclaimed. And then at the last moment, he slid sideways off the ball, falling onto his bum. The ball went rolling across the floor.

Una, Aoléon's little sister, was about half Aoléon's height. She had a rounded face with cheeks like peaches and extra-large blue eyes just like those of her older sister. Una started giggling at Gilbert and could not stop despite Aoléon giving her a stern look. Gilbert didn't seem to mind, though, because he was laughing at himself.

"Ok, I got it this time for sure." Gilbert got up once again, retrieved the ball and sat down very delicately. Everything was working great until he decided to reach over the table to grab a slice of pizza.

"Success!" Gilbert exclaimed as he clutched the pizza slice, bringing it back to his plate while licking his lips. But then his weight shifted slightly, and the ball slipped out from under him causing his legs to kick up toward the ceiling as he fell over backward. His pizza slice flew high into the air and landed on his face. Zoot, Aoléon's pet, ran over to where Gilbert lay on the ground and began to lick his face where the pizza had landed.

"Uuuck! Gedda-off-a-me!" Gilbert exclaimed.

"BREEET!" trilled Zoot.

Una, unable to contain herself any longer, burst into fits of laughter, and Aoléon's cheeks turned bright blue as she tried to keep herself from laughing along with her. Phobos and Deimos, Aoléon's parents, gave them both stern looks. Aoléon grimaced, then sent a telepathic command to Zoot urging him to go to his room. Zoot obeyed reluctantly, giving Aoléon a forlorn look of disappointment as he left the dining room area. Gilbert laughed at himself, smiled at Aoléon, and picked himself back up off the floor, wiping the pizza off his face with his sleeve.

"My hockey coach once told me, 'if you don't fall down once in a while, you're not skating hard enough.'" Aoléon grinned, nodding. "Although, somehow I don't think he had this in mind when he told me that," commented Gilbert.

Gilbert eventually got the hang of balancing on the ball and finally took a bite of his pizza, which to Gilbert's surprise, turned out to be tasty indeed. It wasn't nearly as good as a New York pizza or one from Nebraska for that matter (which is all that Gilbert had ever tasted), but he was very hungry, and in his mind, it sure beat a stick in the eye, starving to death, or worse — having to eat that liquefied Martian galact stuff.

"Please tell us about your home world Gilbert," said Deimos.

"Well sir, I live on a farm in a place called Nebraska. There are wheat and cornfields that go as far as the eye can see, and a whole lotta cattle. Life in Nebraska can get kinda boring though. Besides school, sports, and my chores, there isn't a lot to do there."

"Are there any questions you might have for us?" inquired Deimos.

Gilbert turned toward Aoléon. "Aoléon, when we flew in your saucer from Earth, I could see strange lights and colors. What were they?"

"What you saw was a hyper-spacial distortion that occurs when you transition beyond superluminal speed."

"But I thought that going faster than light was impossible."

"Who says?"

"Einstein said it, I think. He said it would be impossible to travel faster than the speed of light."

"I can try to explain, but it is extremely technical and quite boring…and because I am neither a scientist nor an engineer, I may not be able to explain it to you properly."

"I'm really curious!"

"Well okay, then I will try. Are you aware of the five basic forms of matter?"

"They taught us about four forms of matter in school — never heard of a fifth," responded Gilbert, perplexed.

"It is possible that your science is not advanced enough yet to have discovered the fifth form of matter. You will have to take my word for it," explained Aoléon. "It is the fourth form of matter — plasma — that concerns us when we are talking about superluminal travel. Do you really want me to bore you with all the details?" inquired Aoléon. "It is quite tedious — we could have more fun sitting around watching metal oxidize."

"Sure. Please go on."

"Well…okay then, I will do my best to explain. The five naturally occurring states of matter are solid, liquid, gas, plasma and beam. We will ignore the fifth state of matter, beam, as well as all other artificially induced forms of matter and focus on the fourth state of matter — plasma. Plasma is the most common form of matter in the universe, and it is important for certain physical conditions that can be used, for example, to — how should I express this to you? — to generate antigravity. That is an inaccurate Terran term because there really is no such thing, but I use it because there is no better substitute in your language, given your people's extremely primitive level of scientific understanding."

"Ouch! Remember, us 'primitive' humans have highly advanced egos that bruise easily."

Aoléon giggled. "Essentially, there are no bipolar forces — for example, positive and negative or gravity and antigravity as your scientists currently believe. But, rather, only observer-dependent reflective behavior of a single, large unified force at different levels. With antigravity or, more accurately, the displacement of gravitational characteristics into levels, one can, for example, cause apparently solid matter to levitate. This method is employed partly by us and partially by other extraterrestrials as a means of propulsion for our spacecraft."

"Sorry, but what is a level?

"A level has to do with how matter and energy are the same thing — waveforms that 'vibrate' at specific 'frequencies' that are grouped into levels. The higher the level, the higher the 'vibratory frequency.' Again, I use the words 'vibratory frequency' as a crude substitute because there are no words in your language to describe this phenomenon accurately."

"And what about other dimensions? Do they exist?"

"Not the way you might think of them. Dimensions are a mathematical construct. Your scientists have misused the term to describe alternate universes with alternate physical realities. We Martians describe these alternate universes as 'spheres of influence' or 'bubbles.' The omniverse is broken up into foam. Foam is comprised of many bubbles, and each bubble contains several layers. In one of the layers in one of the bubbles that make up the foam of the omniverse is what you know as third-density-level physical reality. Are you with me so far?"

"Yes, please go on," said Gilbert. "I think I am beginning to understand."

"Good! Now, the illusion of third-density 'solid' matter, such as yourself and any object, has certain properties that reside in each layer. There is something like an informational layer, 'metadata' for solid matter if you will, that governs the physical third-density layer and is what we use to perform various psionic tasks — for example, kinetic movement or levitation."

"So you're saying that the universe is like a giant bubble bath?"

Aoléon giggled. "It is like you say. There are many spheres of influence that form a foam-like structure similar to one of your soapy bubble baths."

"But, how do you make this plasma?"

"Do you remember the small metal sphere that you touched when you first entered my craft back on Terra?"

"How could I forget?! When I touched it, I thought I might have radiated myself or something."

"That is the ship's fusion reactor, and it is perfectly safe. It generates a special form of radiation that is used to bombard copper at the right angle to create what your scientists call 'antimatter.' The 'antimatter' is then converted to produce a gravimetric displacement field used in levitation and propulsion."

"So the reactor creates some kind of force field that goes around your ship?"

"Indeed. When the field is stable, you just *think* where you want to go, and you *go*. We move at the speed of thought."

"This sounds like magic to me."

"Magic in your language means any 'unexplained phenomenon,' does it not? If you could take one of your jet aircraft from today and fly it say, one thousand years ago during your so-called 'middle ages,' would they not think it was magic, too?"

"They probably would."

"But you know better, right? You know it is *not* magic, just advanced science that enables you to fly in your airplanes."

"I think I understand."

"I did not realize that Terrans could be so smart."

"Gee, thanks Aoléon." Gilbert blushed. "But I'm not so sure. My teachers would probably disagree because I am getting mostly Cs and Bs in school."

"After you get back from Mars, you will be able to teach *them* something!"

"How did you learn all this?"

"I am actually not very smart…well, compared to some. But I do have a direct telepathic link to a crystal-holokronic datastore that houses most of our people's collected knowledge. Because we are primarily a telepathic race, most of our knowledge can be easily shared."

"Not very smart?!" Gilbert chuckled. "On Earth, you would probably be considered a genius. It must be difficult to keep secrets or lie when you can read another person's mind."

"Indeed."

"On Earth, we like our privacy. I think having others being able to read your thoughts would be too much for most of us."

"A telepathic connection creates absolute transparency in communication. Although it is still possible to block others from reading our own thoughts, we cannot lie because everyone else would know it immediately," replied Phobos, Aoléon's mother.

"I wonder what life on Earth would be like if no one could lie to each other. My mom would always know without asking if I'd done my homework or not. Now that is a scary thought!"

"Right! Whenever I do something wrong, my mom seems to know about it almost instantly," said Aoléon with a wink. "This is because telepathic communication is instantaneous over any distance."

After dinner, Aoléon showed Gilbert to her room, which he was surprised to see was empty.

"Are you ready to begin your sleep cycle? I can sense your exhaustion." She waved her arm and where the opaque metallic wall once was, a window appeared. The metal of the wall turned transparent, giving Gilbert a view outside. Suddenly, with a second wave of Aoléon's hand, two sleep pods materialized out of nowhere.

"How did you do that?"

"Holokronic matter converter," replied Aoléon. "If the sleep chamber is not comfortable enough for you, I can materialize a different one."

"I don't understand, how can a hologram become a solid object?"

"You mean you do not know already? Terrans are known throughout the galaxy as being the most remarkable in terms of manifesting third-density reality."

"What are you talking about?"

"Tell me what things you have at home in your sleep chamber."

"You mean my bedroom? Well, I have my bed, my telescope, some toys, some posters, and my dresser and desk."

"And when you leave your room, do your things remain there?"

"That's a silly question. Of course they are still there!"

"For us, that is not the case. After we leave, all of our holo-objects dematerialize, unless of course they are sustained by a holokronic device."

"You're kidding! That's ridiculous!" Gilbert chortled. "On second thought, my socks do sometimes have a habit of disappearing without me knowing about it. So maybe you do have a point."

"One of the things that makes Terrans incredibly special among all other sentient life in the galaxy is just that! The objects you manifest can maintain third-density form even when you are not present in the same room or space. This is *most* remarkable to us."

"That's just crazy talk! It's normal!"

Aoléon smiled at Gilbert and motioned for him to climb into the sleep chamber. Gilbert was so exhausted from the day's activities that he fell asleep almost immediately.

⊙⊙⊙

LOWER FEEB DISTRICT ENCLAVE
MARTIAN MEGALOPOLIS
OLYMPUS MONS
PLANET MARS

Bizwat flew toward his second delivery in the Feeb District, an enclave in the lower depths of the megalopolis where alien lowlifes (off-worlders, mostly non-Martian in origin), dregs, miscreants, rapscallions, scoundrels, and various other forms of alien ne'er-do-wells from all over the galaxy came to conduct mostly illegal business or to be entertained. The farther away from the galactic center you got, the more likely you would run into these shady types of aliens. Mars, being in the Sol System far out on one of the spiral arms of the Milky Way Galaxy and near the galactic rim, was one of many hotbeds for illegal-alien activities.

Bizwat arrived at his destination, an alleyway behind Emo's Paradise, one of the hottest underground clubs in the lower Feeb enclave. The music was loud and thumping, even outside in the alleyway, and he could hear the low bass-crunching sound of a sonic axe playing a heavy riff. He stepped out of his velocipod and checked the time on the smartbox platter container, which told him he had arrived with ten cycles to spare. He scanned the alleyway and noticed a stretched charipod hovering just outside the rear exit door to the club. Bizwat walked over to it and tapped on the extended canopy. It slid back to reveal a Martian wearing a glow-in-the-dark costume and sandwiched between two attractive, scantily clad, female Martian dancers.

"I am looking for Andromeda Supernova. He ordered a pizza," Bizwat said to the Martian in the back of the charipod.

"Right. That would be me," said Andromeda Supernova as he leaned forward smiling. "Just in time, too! We are between sets, and it is almost time to go back on stage."

"Twenty chits please."

"Right-O! Here you GO!" said Andromeda Supernova. "Hey, I'm a poet and didn't know it. Keep the change."

"Thank you, sir," said Bizwat as he handed him the platter. The two girls ogled Bizwat in his Procyon outfit and giggled. The dome to the charipod closed, and Bizwat headed back to his velocipod.

A moving reflection in the velocipod's canopy caught his eye — a seven-foot-tall Ataien insectoid clutching a nerve disruptor in its left pincer was coming up behind him. Bizwat quickly scanned the being's thoughts. The Ataien and his friends were malcontents: a renegade gang of Ataien mercenary thugs from Epsilon Eridani. Bizwat pretended he was unaware of them and opened the canopy to his velocipod.

The Ataien he had seen in the canopy reflection walked right up behind him. "Gimme all your chits!" screeched the insectoid through a vocoder that instantly translated its guttural clicking, screeching and popping sounds into Galactic Standard.

"I cannot give you what is not mine," replied Bizwat, still facing away from the insectoid. He faced the group. "I do have some platters, which I will gladly hand over — if you are hungry."

"Galact platters? Ugh! I would rather chew on the ass end of a Sukr'ath! Now gimme your pod, Martian scum!" screeched the insectoid mercenary.

"My mistake. I forgot that bugs only consume excrement," Bizwat smirked. "Let me introduce you to my two best friends — my pair of insect lobotomizers. I nullified many a bug with them." Bizwat raised his arms and the crystal amulets affixed to the sleeves of his Procyon armor glowed. Psionic energy amplified by the crystals created two coherent psi-plasma blades that arced outward like coronal discharges. "Lucky for you, I happen to be in a good mood tonight; so I give you this final warning. Buzz away before I swat you."

"Swat me?" replied the Ataien with a chuckle. But before his friends could either laugh or move, Bizwat spun around, angled his blades, and sliced through the air so fast that his body was a blur of light. Two of the insectoids that had been

standing on either side of Bizwat let out a shriek and fell backward; their pistols exploded in their hands.

"No!" screeched the remaining insectoid in its own language as it squeezed the trigger and fired at Bizwat. Bizwat's body blurred. He sidestepped the blast and activated the cloaking shield on his Procyon body armor, making him nearly invisible.

At the same time that he activated his cloak, he used telepathy to project a false mental image into the Ataien's mind, making him think that his partner was Bizwat. The Ataien fired at the false image and shot his partner instead. Bizwat focused his psionic power to heat and transmute the metal in the plasma pistol of the Ataien to his left so that the weapon misfired.

Bizwat phase-matter jumped directly in front of the mercenary, instantly covering fifty feet of distance. Before the insectoid could react, the pistol exploded in its hand, having been sliced in two by Bizwat's psi-blade. Bizwat kicked the insectoid so hard in the thorax that he sailed across the alleyway and hit the wall, knocking him unconscious. The cloaking shield on Bizwat's Procyon body armor flicked off, returning him to full visibility.

Bizwat took a deep breath. *"Amateurs,"* he growled and deactivated his psi-blades.

"Bravo!" cheered Andromeda Supernova who stepped out of his charipod and applauded. The two female Martian dancers beside him giggled with delight. "Well done. Well done," he beamed. "Let me offer you two passes to my next performance. I'll be opening next week at the megalopolis Galactic Arena for the Black Holes. You can't miss it!"

"Cheers," said Bizwat as he scanned the tickets into his wrist-portable omnitool. The two girls smiled at him as Bizwat got back into his velocipod and took off for his last delivery of the night.

MARTIAN SPACE ACADEMY

CHAPTER EIGHT

MARTIAN SPACE ACADEMY
MARTIAN MEGALOPOLIS
OLYMPUS MONS
PLANET MARS

It was morning, and Gilbert and Aoléon flew to the Martian Space Academy on her skyboard. Aoléon soared rapidly past various buildings and through the inside of some of the much larger arcologies. The arcologies were enormous, raised-pyramid hyperstructures — self-contained micro-cities in a single, enormous building. They combined high population density residential habitats with self-contained commercial, food, agricultural, waste, energy, and transportation facilities — everything you could need to live in comfort on a planet mostly devoid of arable land, plant and wildlife.

Aoléon avoided swarms of saucer traffic, finally landing on the platform in front of her school. The Martian Space Academy campus comprised a complex of buildings situated on a raised city platform. It was an impressive sight to behold.

"Let me guess…SWEET!" giggled Aoléon as Gilbert stared wide-eyed at the building before him.

"Er…actually, how about…*this — oozes — awesomeness!*"

They both laughed as Aoléon stowed her board at the entrance to the academy. She wiggled out of her spacesuit, revealing her yellow miniskirt and top, and then pulled on her boots. "You knew I was about to say that!" Students were streaming in through the main entrance, and Gilbert noticed that many of them looked different from the rest of the Martians he had seen.

"Are those students Martians?" Gilbert inquired, motioning toward a group resembling purple spotted octopi. The main difference between these beings and, say, an Earth octopus, is that these beings possess a large cycloptic eye in the center of their heads.

"No, not all are Martian. Some are students from other planets and star systems. They are what you might call on Terra 'exchange students.' Those two over there, for example, are Neptunian. They evolved inside the planet-wide oceans of Neptune. I believe the cuttlefish and the Neptunians may actually be distant cousins."

"Zoikers!" exclaimed Gilbert.

"But unlike the octopi and cuttlefish, most sentient alien species typically are humanoid life forms such as you and me: with two arms, two legs, and a head with two eyes, a nose, and a mouth."

Aoléon motioned for Gilbert to follow her into the building. They entered a giant metallic blue atrium and headed toward several gravtubes. Gilbert followed Aoléon into a tube and was lifted into the air by an invisible gravimetric force field. They levitated without any support, making Gilbert uneasy. The transparent gravtube shot them upwards at an incredible speed, briefly giving Gilbert an overview as they passed by of the atrium below and the various floors.

They quickly arrived at their floor. Gilbert was unsure of which floor because he had lost count. He followed Aoléon out of the tube into an atrium. Here and there groups of students were clumped together talking. Some of the students were short and skinny Martians, some had short furry bodies resembling bears, others looked like bipedal insects, and yet others resembled cephalopods — like the Neptunians, shuffling along on their tentacles.

"Hi, Aoléon," one Martian girl called out. Gilbert noticed that she was shorter than Aoléon and was wearing a colorful purple, orange, yellow, and silver suit with purple boots.

"Hello, Emuu," Aoléon said. "I would introduce you to my new friend, Gilbert, but I have to run. We are late for class." Gilbert also noticed that many of Aoléon's classmates, especially the guys, were watching her and Emuu intently.

"See you later," Emuu hurriedly responded.

"Follow me," Aoléon turned to Gilbert. "We have Martian Anthropology first with Plutarch Xenocrates." As they walked toward the first class, Aoléon bumped into another Martian girl who had two friends in tow. She was wearing a bright purple and gold hexagon-patterned outfit with purple boots. Gilbert glanced up from her boots to see the girl smirking at him.

"Aoléon, I have not seen you in a while," sneered the girl.

"Well, hello Charm," responded Aoléon, half-smiling.

"So who is the nurb in the old spacesuit?" sneered Charm.

"A friend," Aoléon replied coldly as she read Charm's thoughts, anticipating what was to come next.

"A little drafty in the classroom today, is it?" She peered over at Gilbert. "Or let me guess…your family cannot afford a simple holokronic-matter converter, and you have nothing left to wear?!" Her two friends chuckled. (For Martians, holokronic-matter converters reside in every home and are as common as the proverbial toaster back on Earth.)

Aoléon frowned, slightly crinkling up her nose. Gilbert turned to Aoléon, eyebrows raised.

"Gilbert, this is Charm Lepton. Charm, Gilbert. And that is her best friend, Quarkina. You could say they are an inseparable…a nucleonic pair because they never are apart," Aoléon added with a light chuckle. "They even wear the same clothes."

Gilbert glanced down. "Holy NERTS!" he blurted, then blushed. "Er, I mean, nice outfits."

"Very funny. So where were you after class yesterday? You were not studying in the conservatory like you usually do." Charm grinned like a cat that had just trapped a mouse.

"I went for a little joyride. What of it?" Aoléon glanced away as if she were bored.

"Oh, I see. You were flying around making crop circles again in your parents' junker?" sneered Charm.

Aoléon's lips tightened. "The ship is not a piece of junk," she said, clenching her fist.

"Oh, yes it is. And you are lucky the Xiocrom did not catch you. I understand that we get extra chits this month for turning people in!" Charm goaded her.

"You would not!" Aoléon protested.

"I might!" The tone of her voice struck Aoléon like an icy spike driven by malice. Another thought caused a smirk, and her voice softened. "I guess that is all you can afford, 'cause your daddy is just a common factory worker," Charm sneered while her friends laughed behind her back. "Oh I just hope he does not get blown up or something. That would be horrible now, would it not?"

"What do you mean blown up?!"

"Never mind!"

Brief flashes, images and feelings flooded through Aoléon's mind as she caught a glimpse into Charm's thoughts. Just before Charm blocked the telepathic link between them, she saw visions of the factory where her father worked, destroyed. She also sensed that something had gone terribly wrong with Charm's parents and that they had something to do with Charm's sudden hostility toward her. However, the telepathic link was cut before Aoléon could discover what had gone wrong.

Charm's expression changed as if she had just tasted something very sour. Her two friends stopped chuckling and glared at Aoléon.

After a moment, Charm managed to regain her façade of strength. "What's the matter? Did some asteroids clog up that black hole you call a brain?" retorted Charm.

Aoléon half-smiled. "Compared to me, you are the queen of the encephalographically challenged. And yes, my saucer may be old, but I cannot complain because at least I have one."

"Ahh, But I *do* have one — a brand new saucer that daddy got me just the other day. It is hovering just out front…top of the line, totally tricked out with state-of-the-art gravimetric-displacement drive, holokronic display, the latest generation of A.I., and telepathic sound system. I do not even have my permit yet, but father knew I needed something to learn on."

"How about we settle this with a race? You in your new saucer that your daddy bought you and me on my skyboard?" Aoléon replied calmly. Gilbert chuckled loudly, barely containing his laughter.

"A race? All right then, see you after school."

"Tomorrow after school. Today is a game day," added Aoléon. "I have a psi-ball match, as you know very well." Charm and her friends scowled and then brushed past Gilbert. Charm accidentally tripped over his boot and fell, causing her friends to fall, as well. Aoléon could barely contain her laughter. Gilbert smiled. Charm and her friends got up quickly and sped off down the hall toward class. Gilbert and Aoléon continued after them.

"'Sup with her?"

"She thinks she is better than everyone else. And for some reason, her vibratory frequency is extremely low — she seems more troubled than usual. Come. We are going to be late."

Aoléon and Gilbert entered Plutarch Xenocrates' Martian Anthropology class and headed toward the back of the room. They took their seats next to the other students, including some from various alien races who sat chatting among themselves. The classroom was oviform with austere bluish-grey, mercury-hued walls. Holokronic projection desks and spherical chairs arranged in arcing rows completed the classroom furniture. Large prolate portal windows faced the vast expanse of the megalopolis. Outside, streams of saucer traffic flew by neighboring buildings that stretched as far as the eye could see.

As Gilbert sat down next to Aoléon, he noticed his holokronic spherical chair form inviting him to sit. The chair then adjusted itself to his bottom. The holokronic desk had a display on it with Martian glyphs that he couldn't read.

Plutarch Xenocrates motioned to the class to get their attention. He was unusually tall for a Martian, with long slender arms, legs and fingers. His head looked like it had been squashed and stretched by a heavy weight, yet he had a kind face.

He seems friendly enough, thought Gilbert — *at least on the surface.*

His greyish-blue eyes peered through Gilbert as if he could read the depths of his soul. Quickly averting his eyes, Gilbert wondered if he could read his mind as Aoléon could.

Just thinking the wrong thing could get us in trouble. Aoléon smiled, sensing his thoughts, and Gilbert exhaled deeply, his tight shoulders relaxing a bit as he sat back into his chair.

Plutarch Xenocrates began the class by taking attendance, calling each student's name one by one. They raised their hands (or the appropriate tentacle in some cases) to signal their presence. "I would like to introduce to the class two Neptunian exchange students. Izmani and Zelda, please stand up." The exchange students rose up from their desks by extending their tentacles onto the floor. A mucus-like fluid residue oozed out, staining the floor. Their tentacles awkwardly pushed and slid their bodies forward. Each of the Neptunian students had a single, oversized, cycloptic eyeball in the center of her head, a large mouth that took up a good part of her midsection, and eight dangly tentacles.

Ionium, a Martian boy sitting near Gilbert, made a wise-crack to a Martian girl sitting across from him. "Hey Daedalia, she is not from Neptune, I bet she is from URANUS!" His buddy Ascuris, sitting next to him, sputtered and laughed as some galact he had been drinking snorted out of his

nose. Several other classmates joined in laughing out loud at the Neptunian girl. Zelda hid her face in her tentacles. Her natural yellow skin tone shifted to a dark blue, and her spots glowed bright purple. She lifted herself up using her tentacles and began to shuffle slowly toward the portal. Her skin transformed again, now becoming translucent as she quietly slid out of the classroom.

"That joke is older than you are, you brainless space slug!" spat Zelda's twin sister Izmani as she slid out of the room after her sister.

"Space slug! Look who is talking!" retorted Ionium.

"That is enough," rebuked the plutarch. "Izmani and Zelda are our guests, and I expect you to treat them with respect." A few moments later, Zelda slid back into the classroom after attending to her sister. No one made a sound.

"Because we have several off-world visitors in our class today, I think it would be appropriate to take a day to learn more about the history of Mars and how we got here. So we are going to take a look at the ancient period in Andromedan history called 'The Great Diaspora' and how it led to the colonization of Mars and the creation of Martian society as it exists today. The good news for those of you who are rolling your eyes because you are already familiar with this material is that we are going to take a short field trip to the Galactic History Museum. It should be a nice change of pace. Now everyone please follow me." Whispers of excitement filled the room as the students shuffled through the door.

Plutarch Xenocrates led the class down the hall to the gravtubes where they shot upward to a shuttlecraft landing zone. The class boarded an academy shuttle that took them to the Galactic History Museum near the center of the Martian megalopolis, not far from the giant citadel that was the Luminon's palace. The class exited the shuttle on a landing pad that was close to the main entrance of the museum.

Gilbert had never imagined such a strange and splendid place. The museum was a colossal domed building with windows crafted out of a blue metallic alloy similar to the rest of the buildings in the megalopolis. Intricate, vine-like swirling patterns carved into the metal shifted in hue as they walked past. Gilbert, Aoléon and the rest of the class made their way to the entrance where Gilbert observed several large holograms of Martian historical figures positioned around the entrance. As Gilbert passed them, each figure turned to watch the class pass by, and some even talked, greeting them with the traditional Andromedan Fibonacci spiral wave. The class followed Plutarch Xenocrates through the main doors into an atrium that led to another room containing several exhibits about ancient Andromedan history.

Yenyech, an exchange student who came from one of Jupiter's moons, resembled a blobby, translucent, gelatinous mass. The Martian dust frequently made him sneeze. "Ah — chooo!" This time, he got Zugak, a Viagraa'n from the seventh planet in the Asellus Primus system located in the Boötes constellation, spraying huge amounts of alien mucus all over its face. Zugak wiped off the mucus from its face with a tentacle.

"This one needs he-lp...Cannot-con-trol-an-ger-any-long-ger." Zugak sputtered as it turned from yellow to red and started to expand like a balloon. Zugak was a creature composed of a head and body made of several gasbags of various sizes, which enabled it to float freely in its home world.

Zugak exploded like a collection of overblown balloons, shooting upward into the air and quickly spinning around while bouncing off the walls and ceiling. Finally, it settled back down to the ground, wiped some of the mucus off its face with one of its tentacles and flew out of the room shrieking.

"That guy is a little off," Gilbert quietly commented to Aoléon.

"He is a Viagraa'n...they get easily excited."

"Shall we begin now?" asked Plutarch Xenocrates, his lips tightening. Xenocrates waved his arm, and a giant three-dimensional holokronic projection of the Milky Way Galaxy materialized before them. It zoomed into one area of the Milky Way — Gilbert recognized it immediately from his astronomy studies as the constellation Andromeda.

Plutarch Xenocrates lectured as the images played out on the holokron in front of them.

"Does anyone know what was the first sentient species to achieve interstellar space travel?" There was an audible pause as Plutarch Xenocrates waited. "Anyone?"

"Uh, we did?" said one Martian boy.

Plutarch Xenocrates shook his head. "Anyone else?"

"The Draconian race, the biggest party-poopers in the Galaxy," joked Phrixi, a Martian girl.

"Intergalactic bullies of the universe," added Nilus, a Martian boy. The class laughed.

"You were not supposed to use telepathy. But nonetheless, yes, you are correct. Ancient Andromedan mythology tells us that about four billion years ago, a hostile sentient reptiloid species known as the Draconians were deposited into this bubbleverse from another via a black hole."

As the plutarch spoke, a holographic image appeared in Gilbert's mind, showing a black hole emerging from the void of space with thousands of ships flying out of it.

Gilbert was startled at first but then realized that these images were being telepathically shared with the entire class.

"The alien race that brought the reptiloids into our bubbleverse — known as the Forerunners, or in the ancient Draconian dialect the 'Paa'Tal' — are largely unknown to us. However, we have found evidence of their existence in certain monuments and ancient relics left scattered throughout the galaxy — some of which can be found right here on Mars. What we believe happened was that the Paa'Tal essentially removed all reptiloid life forms from their universal bubble and dumped them into ours. We believe there had been an ancient conflict between the Dracs and the Paa'Tal, and the Paa'Tal had won."

The plutarch eyed Gilbert directly as he finished his sentence, and Gilbert quickly averted his eyes. Gilbert felt uneasy, as if he were being singled out in some way, and his fears of being discovered bubbled to the surface.

The plutarch continued as if nothing had happened. "The Draconian reptiloids settled in the Orion constellation and formed what is now known as the Orion Group — on their home world of Alpha Draconis (Akahn in Draconian), which orbits around the super-giant star Beta Orionis (Rigel). They also formed major colonies on Alpha Orionis (Betelgeuse) and Gamma Orionis (Bellatrix) with several minor colonies on the lesser stars Mintaka, Alnilam and Alnitak.

Flash. The classroom disappeared, and Gilbert was floating in space. Bursts of holographic images flew through Gilbert's mind, and instantly he was transported. The vision zoomed into the super-giant star, and a vast planetary system emerged, orbiting around it. Gilbert felt a rushing movement once again. As he flew closer to the main star, two smaller stars emerged, and he discovered that the system was, in fact, composed of a trinary star system.

He could now see two much smaller stars (Rigel Beta and Rigel Gamma) that were orbiting around each other. Together, they orbited around the super-giant Rigel Alpha at roughly 2200 AU. Just outside of Rigel Alpha's massive accretion disc (a shell of expelled gas about 80 AU in diameter away from its Rigel Alpha center) starting at about 100 AU, Gilbert could now see thousands of planets orbiting in the system.

Next, Gilbert's mind focused on clustered groups of planets and planetoids that were separated by five distinct asteroid belts. The second asteroid belt was located at 190 AU, located between two habited planets called "Styx" and "Aliakmonas" (Andromedan names because the Draconian counterparts are unpronounceable). This was where Alpha Draconis, the Draconian home world was located.

It was far more than just a vision he was experiencing. It felt as if he had been instantly teleported 800 light-years from Mars and four billion years back in time to a small jungle planet. He felt as if he were actually *there*, experiencing it first hand. His vision was suddenly interrupted, and he was back in class on Mars.

"Can we skip the astronomy lesson and get right to their home world?" inquired one of the Martian students who had seen all this before. A couple of other students nodded to each other in agreement. Plutarch Xenocrates grunted a non-verbal response. He then ignored the fifth asteroid belt and quickly moved on to discuss the Draconian home world — Alpha Draconis.

The image focused on one of the planets in the system (Alpha Draconis) — a lush, jungle-like planet with two great oceans located about 220 AU from Rigel A. On the surface of the planet, Gilbert could see a diversity of plant and wildlife. Most of the planet was either tropical or subtropical, with some of the far northern and southern regions having grass plains similar to Nebraska, Gilbert's home back on Earth.

The holographic image in Gilbert's mind blurred again as they moved under the surface of the planet to reveal a continent-wide underground tunnel and cavern system where the bulk of the Draconian civilization lived. "With more than three billion years or so of evolution, the reptilian species became technologically advanced — being the first to develop interstellar starships with plasma-based weapons technology. They were also unmatched in prowess for genetic engineering. Their technological advancements, coupled with the primary belief that they were the dominant species in the bubbleverse and all others were created to be subservient to them, ultimately led to interstellar war."

"Why did they start the war?" inquired a Martian boy.

"No one really knows for sure why they started the war. However, most believe it was purely for conquest and to secure their position as the dominant species in our Galaxy," replied the plutarch. "For a time, they had a distinct technological and military advantage over most of the other sentient species in the galaxy, and that gave them the upper hand in the war — at least in the beginning. In time, the other species learned to survive, adapt, and eventually to confront and defeat them, but many worlds were lost before that happened."

"Why is he going on and on about this?" Gilbert quietly asked Aoléon.

"He wants to share our history with the new students such as yourself. However, I also sense something else… Some of his thoughts are occluded from me at the moment — wait…I think I sense that he may be concealing something; however, I am unsure why," whispered Aoléon. "He is blocking me."

Gilbert nodded. "Most of my teachers are like that. They try to dump information on us without first explaining why it is important. That is one of the reasons I don't like school very much," said Gilbert, and he returned his attention to the plutarch.

The plutarch continued. "About one hundred twenty million years ago, they began to wage an interstellar war, embarking on a campaign of conquest to capture all other known systems with intelligent life — enslaving the masses, genetically engineering some to serve as slave labor and in some instances as a food source, or nullifying them outright to pillage their natural resources."

"They began by capturing and inhabiting nearby star systems in the Orion constellation, namely Ursa Minor, Ursa Major, and Rigel, among others. As time went on, they expanded outward. At this point, they formed what is now known as the Draconian Empire — sometimes referred to as the Draconian Collective."

"The first contact with our people came when a Draconian mothership visited our home world in the Andromeda constellation. Our ancient records say that our people sent a peaceful greeting message, which they somehow misinterpreted as hostile. They immediately began to glass our home world from orbit, firing their powerful plasma-based weapons systems from their motherships. Billions of our people died in the opening attack, and very few managed to escape."

I wonder what he means by glass their home world? thought Gilbert.

When I say that the planet was glassed, I mean plasma beams scorched the surface of the planet and wiped out all organic life. The oceans evaporated, and the rocks and dirt on the surface were melted into a shiny green glass, responded Plutarch Xenocrates telepathically.

Zoiks! He knows! thought Gilbert. Gilbert was startled by Plutarch Xenocrates' telepathic response to his unspoken question. Aoléon glanced at Gilbert's panicked expression. She smiled, telepathically sending him her γαλήνη (serenity). He immediately relaxed.

Relax my Terran friend. Yes, I know, but I am also on your side. Plutarch Xenocrates winked at Gilbert and then continued with his lecture.

"Our people, being technologically advanced yet peaceful, did not have the military strength to fight back. More than a billion of our people were nullified, and three out of fifteen inhabited planets in the system — Neela, Someka and Aria — were destroyed when the reptiloids used their plasma-based weapons and glassed our home world colonies from orbiting motherships. The Draconians took 250 million as slaves from the remaining fifteen planets. Another half billion of our people escaped in ships and fled to other star systems where they created new colonies. One of those colonies was our settlement here on Mars. Thus ended the first great interstellar war."

Gilbert began to feel a bit paranoid. He gazed around the room at the other students wondering who else might know that he was from Earth. Occasionally another Martian student would look at him for a brief moment, but nothing so far indicated that he had been completely exposed to the class. Even so, he was feeling a bit unnerved. Meanwhile, the Martian professor continued his lecture on the Draconian war with the Andromedan people, yet Gilbert found it hard to concentrate.

"About seventy-five million years ago, the reptiloids came to our system — the Sol System — and colonized a planet known as Phaethon, which used to be situated between Mars and Jupiter, right where the asteroid belt is located today. Once again, conflict between our species broke out, spread to other systems, and eventually included hundreds of races. This was the beginning of the second great interstellar war."

"At that time, Mars was nineteen million miles closer to Terra than it is today. There was a Draconian Orion Group military base on Phaethon, and the Andromeda Confederation destroyed the planet by crashing a moon-sized asteroid into it. The asteroid projectile completely annihilated the planet leaving a belt of rock debris — the asteroid belt — where it sits today. Some of the larger pieces of Phaethon were absorbed by the gravitational pull of Jupiter and Saturn and became moons."

"This action, however, had other major repercussions. As the planet-sized projectile was hurled at Phaethon, it passed too close to Mars. The gravitational pull from the asteroid caused intense perturbations that stripped Mars of most of its atmosphere, caused an axial shift, and pulled Mars nineteen million miles further away from its former orbit around the sun, leaving it where it orbits today. It also caused Uranus to pole shift. As a result, Uranus now spins sideways and in retrograde motion to the sun. At that time on Mars, the planet contained a breathable atmosphere, and great oceans filled with fish, plants, and other abundant life lived on the surface. In that single cataclysmic event, the oceans, the atmosphere, and the climate were destroyed along with most life on the surface."

"I sense that we have a question. Would the Terran like to introduce himself and ask his question?" asked Plutarch Xenocrates. Gilbert could suddenly sense the thoughts of every Martian student in the room who was communicating telepathically with the other students.

There — look!

Where?

In the old space suit.

Did you see his face?

His blue skin...it just flushed pink!

Does he have a disease?!

Is he contagious?

No, I think that is normal for a Terran...his blood must be iron-based instead of copper-based!

Telepathic thoughts flashed through Gilbert's mind. He could understand only a tiny bit of what they were saying because the messages were being sent rapid fire, and many thoughts were overlapping, making it impossible to understand all of them. But he got the gist of it — they were all shocked to see a Terran in their midst.

"Class, please try to relax and make our guest feel welcome," said the plutarch.

Aoléon glanced at Gilbert, giving him an encouraging nod to respond. He swallowed and spoke, "Um…yeah, okay. Hi, my name is Gilbert, and I am from a place called Nebraska on Earth. I am here visiting my new friend, Aoléon. No, I am not contagious, and I am not going to try to eat you. I come in peace…And, my question is, how is it possible to move a planet and use it as a projectile? That seems too incredible to me."

"Nice to meet you, Gilbert, and welcome to Mars and my class. Your question is somewhat technical and a little beyond my area of expertise. However, I will attempt to answer it for you in general terms. The way we can move planetary bodies such as we did with the moon that struck

Phaethon is by manipulating its mass. First, eight mother-ships are positioned around the planetoid, forming a lattice cage configuration. After they are in position, the eight motherships combine their field strengths to create a single, intense, plasma force field around the entire planet, thus reducing its mass. After the planet's mass is reduced, it can easily be moved into a new orbit or shot as a projectile. Does that answer your question?"

"Er…yes it does! Thank you, Mr. Plutarch."

It is just **plutarch**, whispered Aoléon telepathically. *It is a title similar to your 'professor.' 'Xenocrates' is his actual name.*

Oh, I see! whispered Gilbert telepathically back to Aoléon, feeling a little embarrassed.

"It is also important to note that Mars was a very different place back then. We lived on the surface of the planet, and one third was covered with water. The air was breathable, and we had an abundance of wildlife roaming free throughout the planet. Today as you know, most of that is gone. We now live underground in extinct, hollowed-out volcanoes, our air is almost completely unbreathable, and the atmosphere and water have been diminished. The

Martian landscape transformed instantly from a lush, green ecosystem into barren deserts with lava rock and sand."

"When the asteroid stripped the atmosphere from Mars on its way to Phaethon, why did not the atmosphere come back after a period of time?" asked Aethiopis, a Martian boy.

"Does anyone know why?" Plutarch Xenocrates inquired, referring the question to the class.

"It disrupted the electromagnetic field around Mars. Then solar radiation slowly eroded our atmosphere to what it is today," said Aoléon.

"What a teacher's pet," whispered Charm to her friend.

"Nice job, Aoléon. For the next class, I want you all to study the next two entries of the course data and write a two-page essay on the significance of the Draconian invasion and the Andromedan colonization of Mars," said Plutarch Xenocrates as he dismissed the class. "And no, Aethiopis, you cannot copy your friend's essay because I will know."

Shiznat! He read my mind! thought Aethiopis.

Gilbert and Aoléon left Plutarch Xenocrates' class and headed for their next class. "It seems that this makeup disguise you put on me isn't doing any good. Your people can easily read my mind. The game is up," Gilbert said as he removed the helmet to his Martian space suit. "Plutarch Xenocrates saw right through me."

"It was only when you blushed that they saw pink. So it was not completely a waste. However, it seems I may have overreacted a bit. Feel free to remove the makeup if you wish," said Aoléon. "Although you do look cute in blue," she giggled.

Gilbert smiled, blushed a bit pink, and then wiped the blue makeup off his face with the palm of his hand. He then put his helmet back on.

"So, where we going now?"

"Zero-g maneuverability training, or what we cadets informally call *the indoctrination*," Aoléon smiled. "We call it that because many first-timers hurl their galactshakes."

"You mean we get to float around in a wind tunnel?"

"Just wait and see."

☉☉☉
MARTIAN SPACE ACADEMY
MARTIAN MEGALOPOLIS
OLYMPUS MONS
PLANET MARS

They made their way down a corridor to a gravtube that shot them along a curved passageway connecting one of the leg extension hubs of the Martian Space Academy to the main complex. When they stepped out of the tube, Gilbert could see that they were in an atrium that faced a giant transparent bubble.

A group of students formed nearby; an instructor began an overview of the training evolution. "Today we are going to practice zero-g maneuvering without the aid of propulsor packs," announced the instructor.

Izmani and Zelda shook their tentacles with excitement at the thought of being in an environment similar to their home world — free-floating in the gaseous environment of Neptune's thick atmosphere with its gigantic planet-wide ocean.

Charm and two of her friends arrived late and made their way to the head of the group, pushing Aoléon aside and almost causing her to fall over. Gilbert felt the sudden urge to deck Charm, but because she was both a girl and a Martian, he restrained himself. Aoléon, sensing Gilbert's anger, motioned for Gilbert to remain calm. *Remember, try not to draw attention to yourself*, Aoléon reminded Gilbert telepathically. Gilbert grunted, holding back his anger.

"In the event that the gravimetric field on your ship should fail, or you have to make an emergency spacewalk, it is extremely important to know how to maneuver in a zero-g environment," the instructor continued. Now please step forward into the chamber where we will begin our training."

The class moved into the spherical chamber. After everyone was inside, the door shut, and a plasma force field enveloped the room. Gilbert felt himself getting lighter and lighter, and his feet lifted off the floor of the chamber.

To be weightless was a strange feeling — somewhat like floating underwater except without the resistance that would normally hinder his movements. He reached out and grabbed for Aoléon's hand, which she held outstretched, but missed it on his first try and found himself gradually spinning upside down.

Aoléon giggled as Gilbert tried desperately to right himself by swinging his arms. "Help me out here!" Gilbert laughed. He grabbed Aoléon's foot and pulled, causing her to spin as well. Both Aoléon and Gilbert started laughing as they spun around each other. Finally, they grasped each other's hands, which stopped their spinning. Gilbert began to sing a song as he floated around.

"What is that?"

"*Walking on the Moon* — one of my favorite Police songs."

"Your law-enforcement officers sing to you?"

"Oh no! The Police was a 1980s rock group."

"Ooooh! Very nice," Aoléon said, giggling. A moment later she added, "The rhythms are wonderful."

"How could you possibly know that?"

She winked at him and replied, "I just heard the song in your head."

Gilbert looked around and noticed that some students in the class were having fun, but others were turning green. Izmani and Zelda moved through the zero-g space gracefully as if performing a weightless ballet. Charm clutched her stomach, looking ill. As she floated toward Gilbert, Charm kicked him in an attempt to push him away from her, but instead, the kick caused her to spin like a top across the chamber. "Help! H-Help me you worthless Feebs!" Charm cried out as she spun out of control.

Gilbert and Aoléon watched as Charm's face turned from turquoise-blue to aqua-green. Two of her friends, Lia and Riu, finally maneuvered over to her and stopped her spinning, whereby she promptly threw up all over them and all down the front of her shiny new purple and pink Martian spacesuit. The rest of the class cracked up with laughter, and even the instructor had a hard time keeping a straight face.

Charm turned to see the instructor barely containing his laughter, and she exploded into a tantrum. "We get one in every group," the instructor grumbled to himself. Immediately he floated over to help Charm out of the chamber. As she left the room, she continued to wail, blaming the instructor for her mishap and threatening to tell her father, whom she claimed would have him promptly reduced in rank and sent to some remote outpost in the Kuiper Belt where the extent of his responsibilities would be to catalog random asteroids and space debris.

Gilbert winked at Aoléon, and she giggled. "You are supposed to be keeping a low profile, remember?"

"Sorry, I just couldn't resist, especially after seeing her push you earlier. When do we get lunch around here? I'm starving!"

"Come on. Next is midday consumption."

☺☺☺

MARTIAN SPACE ACADEMY MARTIAN MEGALOPOLIS OLYMPUS MONS PLANET MARS

The class was dismissed, and Aoléon and Gilbert headed for the gravtube where they jetted to the central spherical orb that was suspended above the main Martian Academy sports complex. They entered what Gilbert assumed was the cafeteria, or at least the Martian equivalent, which was nothing like he was used to at home.

"Good luck with the psi-ball match today, Aoléon!" said a Martian boy.

"Thank you, Ti. I would like to introduce to you my friend, Gilbert," Aoléon said. "Gilbert, this is Ti'Amat. He is a fourth-year cadet at the academy."

"Greetings, Terran."

"Hello, Ti. Nice to meet you. Psi-ball match?" Gilbert said, glancing at Aoléon.

"An important game today against a rival academy."

"What exactly is psi-ball?"

"Oh, you are in for a real treat!" exclaimed Ti. "It is the greatest game on Mars!"

Aoléon nodded in agreement. "We are playing against the Science Academy, and everyone will be there to watch the match," she added. Gilbert glanced at Aoléon, eyebrows raised. "Come on, and I will tell you all about it while we eat," she said, motioning for them to enter the cafeteria.

"Welcome to the Martian Space Academy's primary food consumption area where every meal is a feast and every feast is a banquet!"

"Really?"

"I wish," she laughed. "The food comes out of those dispensers over there, and it tastes about as bad as it looks — slor excrement. The good news is that the pizza and ice cream are decent, even by Martian standards."

"It's about the same on Earth, except the food comes out of cans instead of tubes. It would seem that bad school food is a constant in the universe." For a brief moment, Gilbert had a twinge of homesickness. His thoughts drifted and he found himself wondering what his friends at home might be doing right now and what they would think if they knew he was on Mars. His stomach growled, bringing him out of his thoughts.

He followed Aoléon into a large, domed room where a line of Martian students floated along on a gravity-displacement walkway that led to a group of food dispensers where robotic arms doled out various food types and placed them on the students' platters. More robotic arms extended down from the ceiling, some handing Gilbert and Aoléon trays as they floated by and placing various types of food on their tray such as galact milk, galact pizza, and for dessert: three scoops of fruit-flavored galact ice cream.

Aoléon and Gilbert made their way to a table where several of Aoléon's classmates were eating. "Everyone, I would like to introduce you to my friend, Gilbert." Aoléon's friends turned around and greeted Gilbert. "This is Aeria, a third-year cadet. Aeolis, also a third-year. Nilus, a fourth-year, is on the psi-ball team with me. Phrixi is also a fourth-year; we have celestial mechanics together. That is Lunae, Nix, Pyrrhae, Sacra, Tholus, Hesperia, Eos, Ceti, and Casius — all third-year cadets and classmates of mine. Gilbert nodded to each of them and said, "Nice to meet you."

"Look over there, Aoléon. The Science Academy team has arrived," said Nilus, Aoléon's psi-ball teammate. Aoléon and Gilbert glanced over and saw a large group of Martian students standing around a table. Gilbert noticed that a few of them looked quite intimidating.

"So tell me about this game of yours, Aoléon," said Gilbert. "I'm anxious to hear about psi-ball."

Aoléon quickly scanned Gilbert's mind for any references to Terran sports. After a brief moment, she replied, "Psi-ball is a sport similar to your Terran games of 'capture the flag' and 'dodge ball.' The main difference is that we play inside a cylindrical suspensor-field game grid using skyboards and propulsor packs. Instead of tagging by hand, we throw psi-balls at each other. There are usually obstacles on both sides of the game grid that act as both protection and concealment from the opposing team. The game can sometimes get quite rough. The psi-ball is made of psionic energy and is caught and thrown using a special glove that acts as a psionic amplification device. Depending on how powerful the throw is, it can either tag you or knock you clear off your skyboard. Professional psi-ball is full contact and an extremely rough sport. As Ti said, you are in for a real treat."

"So what is the object of psi-ball? How do you win?"

"The object of the game is to capture the opposing team's 'flag' or what we call a 'gia' and to return it to your side of the game grid without being struck by the psi-ball."

"What is the psi-ball exactly?" asked Gilbert.

"The psi-ball is a sphere of psionic plasma energy that is thrown at opposing players who try to capture your flag. Players can either strike an opposing player directly, or they can attempt to bank a shot off a suspensor field that surrounds the playing field to hit an opposing player."

"Why would they want to do that?"

"If a player is struck with the psi-ball while on the opposing team's side of the game grid and does not catch the ball, then that player is temporarily removed from the game and placed in a 'holding cell.'"

"If the targeted player catches the ball that was thrown at them, then the one who threw it is placed in a holding cell. That is why you never want to make your throws easy to block or catch. Sometimes I trick the player by using my psionic powers to curve the path of the ball in flight, making it almost impossible to catch. They think the ball is coming right at them, and next thing they know…WHAM! It hits them from the side."

"Awe-freaking-some!"

Gilbert's thoughts drifted back to the several times that he played capture the flag with a bunch of his school friends. The main difference was that they typically played in a wooded field at night, and he and all of his buddies were heavily camo'ed up. They fired bottle rockets at each other that they launched from lacrosse-shaft tubes or PVC pipe as a means of tagging one another. The game typically would last until a neighbor called the police to complain about the racket, at which point Gilbert and all his friends would go into 'SERE' mode (Survival, Evasion, Resistance and Escape). They would melt into the fields and slowly make their way home. Some would have bicycles stashed in the field nearby, and others would have to make the journey home entirely on foot. His thoughts made him miss home. "This sounds like a lot of fun. Will I get to watch the game?"

"Of course."

Gilbert was so hungry that he had no trouble finishing all the food on his tray. He noticed that Aoléon ate several slices of galact platter pizza and, for a change, she decided on some fruity-flavored galact ice cream, the fruit harvested from the hydroponic fruit farms on the planet Pluto.

"It is time for me to get ready for psi-ball." Aoléon and Gilbert headed back to the gravtube where they shot down toward the main sport complex hub. "I am going to get ready for the game. You can watch from over there with the other Space Academy spectators," Aoléon said, pointing to a small crowd of Martians gathering together on the opposite side of the atrium.

Gilbert nodded. "Good luck!" He made the Martian gesture of good tidings, spiraling his arm in an outward

Fibonacci circle around his heart-center. Aoléon smiled and returned the gesture and then walked off toward the women's locker room.

Gilbert positioned himself among the other Martian spectators on a hovering platform that rose up into the air, floating high above the Martian Space Academy athletic arena. As he rose, his stomach lurched; the sudden movement of the levitating grandstand surprised him. The platform came to a stop next to a spherical force field game grid.

He glanced across the open expanse that was to become the playing field and saw another hovering platform on the opposite side of the arena that held visitors from the opposing team's school. He glanced up to see Aoléon along with six teammates flying in on skyboards to thunderous cheers from the crowd. Aoléon and her teammates wore bright blue spacesuits bearing the emblem of the Martian Space Academy.

Gilbert watched Aoléon and her teammates warm up but was momentarily distracted by the entrance of the opposing team. The Science Academy team wore purple spacesuit uniforms and flew around the stadium several times, receiving cheers from those on the hovering platform of the visiting school.

Gilbert watched as Aoléon's team gathered on their skyboards in midair and formed a huddle. Ceti, the captain of Aoléon's team, cleared his throat for silence.

"Okay, άνδρες και γυναίκες," he said, instinctively addressing all male and female Martians on the team but forgetting to include the two non-Martian teammates from Neptune.

"And Neptunians," said Izmani and Zelda, each raising a tentacle.

"And all manner of creature, great and small…," added Tiu, laughing.

"Right! Look sharp! This is galactic huge!" exclaimed Ceti. "We cannot let these Science Academy brainless cephalopods win today!" Aoléon floated next to Ceti and punched him in the shoulder, cutting him off.

"Err…sorry. No offense intended to our tentacled Neptunian teammates."

"No speeches," said Aoléon with a laugh. "Get on with it!"

The arena consisted of many obstacles and barriers that acted as a means of concealment and protection. Two of Aoléon's teammates hid their gia behind two obstacles that were on the far right of their side of the playing grid. The Science Academy did the same, but Gilbert couldn't see where they had placed their pennant. He supposed this was done on purpose so that members of the crowd couldn't help their team by telling them where the opposing team's gia was hidden. Another area was set up to act as the Space Academy's holding cell and was marked by a special spherical holographic beacon that hovered in the air indicating the location of the holding cell. After the pennant was placed and the holding cell set up, Aoléon's team gathered in a huddle once more to discuss their opening strategy.

"We should open with a feint off the line to the right side of the grid and send a scouting patrol over the left side using the diversion as cover," said Aoléon. "I will lead the scouting patrol."

Ceti, the Space Academy Captain, nodded. "Line up!"

The referee, a watcher who had a single cycloptic eyeball, signaled for both teams to line up. The twenty players, ten from each team, took their sides along the line that divided the game grid. Aoléon and three other teammates held back and quietly moved to the far left side. The referee raised an arm and then fired a psi-ball into the air. A glowing blue ball of psionic plasma energy suddenly materialized and burst like a firework over their heads.

Ceti and four other teammates swooped over the line on the right side of the game grid, drawing fire. Three Science Academy players fired psi-balls at the three Space Academy players; two of the shots missed, and one was caught by Ceti. Ophir, the Science Academy cadet who had thrown the caught psi-ball, made his way to the Space Academy's holding cell area, sulking as he went. "One down!" shouted Ceti.

Meanwhile, Aoléon and three other teammates made their way deep into the opposing team's side of the field, searching for the pennant.

"Go Aoléon!" shouted Gilbert gleefully. Gilbert heard a snicker behind him and turned to find Charm with two of her friends standing a few rows behind him. They hadn't noticed Gilbert yet when he overheard Charm say, "She will never know what hit her!" and chuckle. Gilbert sensed that they were plotting something and felt a sudden pang of concern.

Ceti fired a psi-ball at the suspensor field barrier, banking the shot perfectly so that it hit Ina, the attacking Science Academy player from the side. The shot knocked her completely off her skyboard, sending her tumbling hundreds

of feet to the ground. Ina used her suspensor field glove to halt her fall. She then recovered her skyboard and made her way reluctantly to the Space Academy holding cell area.

Meanwhile, Aoléon was able to locate the opposing team's gia but met stiff resistance. Two Science Academy defenders, Artemis and Delos, fired simultaneously at Aoléon. Aoléon spun around on her skyboard, caught one of the psi-balls, and blocked the other by employing a psi-shield barrier. Clutching the psi-ball in her glove, she swung her whole torso and arm around in a blur of motion and launched the psi-ball back at Delos. Delos was struck by Aoléon's shot, and both Artemis and Delos headed for the Space Academy's holding cell area. Seeing that the Science Academy's pennant was now unguarded, Aoléon swooped in to capture the gia.

The crowd around Gilbert erupted with cheers. Gilbert turned and noticed Charm smirking at him while motioning toward Aoléon. Gilbert turned back to see Aoléon flying around various obstacles, avoiding fire, and making her way toward her side of the field.

"The Space Academy takes possession of the gia!" cried the announcer.

"Watch this!" Charm exclaimed to one of her friends. Gilbert overheard her and turned to see Charm activate a device she held in her hand. Gilbert tried to warn Aoléon telepathically, but it was already too late.

Two defending players fired psi-balls at Aoléon. Aoléon quickly employed a psionic shield barrier to block the first psi-ball. Just before the second psi-ball was about to strike her, the nacelle on her skyboard exploded, causing her to lose her balance. The second psi-ball struck her with tremendous force, sending her flying. She tumbled headfirst through the air, somersaulting toward the ground a thousand feet below.

Gilbert, panicked with fear at seeing Aoléon fall, leaned forward over the edge of the hovering platform to see if he could spot her. He heard laughter behind him and turned to see Charm with two of her friends laughing and congratulating themselves.

"Aoléon has fallen off her skyboard due to some unforeseen technical problem," said the announcer. "The Science Academy regains control over their gia."

At the last moment, Aoléon deployed her gravity displacement glove to halt her fall. She landed safely on the track field nearly one thousand feet below the game grid. Gilbert turned, hearing snickering directly behind him.

"Did Aoléon have problems with her junky little skyboard?" goaded Charm. "She should take more care next time," she cackled.

"So you did sabotage it!" Gilbert fought the temptation to turn around, grab Charm by her scrawny little neck and toss her off the platform. He held himself back, knowing it would make more trouble than it was worth for himself and Aoléon. Instead, he ignored her, peering over the ledge of the floating grandstand to see if Aoléon was okay.

"Fortunately, she seems to have landed safely," spoke the announcer. "The Space Academy calls time out."

Ceti flew down to Aoléon and lifted her up onto his board. They flew up to the grandstand where the team gathered into a huddle. Gilbert ran over to where Aoléon and her teammates stood.

"Are you okay? Quite a fall you took."

"I am fine, but unfortunately I am going to need a new board," Aoléon said shaking her head. "I just had my skyboard completely overhauled. My nacelle should not have blown."

"I believe it was Charm."

"What do you mean?"

"I overheard a conversation with her and her friends and noticed that she had some kind of device in her hand. I think it acted as some kind of remote to cause the skyboard's nacelle to explode."

"We do not have time for this," said Ceti, cutting off Aoléon. "We are about to begin play, and we need you back on the field. Can you borrow a skyboard from one of the second-stringers?"

Aoléon turned and asked her teammates, one of whom reluctantly lent her his board for the duration of the game. Aoléon thanked the boy and returned to the huddle.

Ceti joined them. "I think it is time to let loose 'Wing Attack Plan Theta!'" she exclaimed.

"Is it that bad?" inquired Ptolemy.

"I am afraid it is," Aoléon said, nodding. All of them turned to stare at Zelda. "These guys are good! We need a breakout play to capture their gia. We need something with a diversion that suckers them into focusing their defensive forces away from our main attack."

"Oh, no! I am not going to be the target again!" Zelda exclaimed, shaking her tentacles. "Last time I spent a week in medical just to recuperate from all the bruises."

"It is the only way. We need a diversion and you make the perfect target," replied Ceti.

"But why is it I have to be the decoy?! I still have bruises from the last time we played." Aoléon and the others glanced down at Zelda's body, featuring squid-like tentacles and yellowish skin with sprinkled spots. But no one could really tell the difference between her spots and a bruise. "Cannot someone else be a decoy this time?"

Her teammates shook their heads and took their positions along the demarcation line, ready to engage Wing Attack Plan Theta. Zelda reluctantly moved into position along the line.

Meanwhile, as Aoléon and her teammates conversed in the huddle, Gilbert noticed Charm and her friends leaving the arena with slumped shoulders and scowls on their faces. Gilbert cracked a smile. Their ploy to sabotage Aoléon's skyboard and remove her from the game had failed.

The referee shot a psi-ball into the air, signaling the game to resume. Zelda flew over the line, attracting the opposing team's fire. Aoléon and Ceti flew toward the Science Academy's gia. Simultaneously, on the opposite side of the game grid, four Science Academy cadets headed toward the Space Academy's gia zone. Zelda barely made it back over the demarcation line after taking three psi-ball hits that almost knocked her unconscious.

Meanwhile, Aoléon and two other Space Academy cadets sped across the line on the far end of the game-grid and headed for the Science Academy's gia. At the same time, the Science Academy's captain, Oki-Nu and three of his teammates — Ophir, Parváa, and Phaethontis — headed for the Space Academy's gia holding area. Oki-Nu, Parváa, Ophir, and Phaethontis reached the gia first and grabbed it while Izmani, Xanthe and Zephyria — Space

Academy defenders — hurled psi-balls at them. Ophir and Phaethontis smartly took the hits, shielding Oki-Nu and allowing him to head back toward the center demarcation line carrying the Space Academy's gia.

"The Science Academy has taken possession of the Space Academy's gia," spoke the announcer. "Oki-Nu passes the gia to Parváa, his wing-man. Parváa passes it back to the Science Academy cadet Delos where he is intercepted by the Space Academy third-year cadet, Ares!"

Ares flew a loop-de-loop on his skyboard after having defended his gia from capture. He returned it back to the gia area on the far side of the game grid. Delos was escorted to the holding cell area.

Meanwhile, Aoléon and Ceti had reached the Science Academy gia area and had snatched the gia. They were now heading back toward the demarcation line as fast as they could, dodging multiple psi-ball attacks from all angles.

"Yeah! Go Aoléon!" shouted Gilbert as Aoléon shot down the field toward the midline. She fired a psi-ball at Phrixi, a Science Academy defender. Aoléon used her psionic power to corkscrew the ball through the air where it struck Phrixi's psionic barrier wall, knocking Phrixi off her skyboard and sending her cartwheeling through the air.

Aoléon didn't stop. She crossed the line with the gia, barely avoiding several psi-ball attacks. She raised the gia high over her head and made a victory lap around her end of the game-grid while Aoléon's teammates flew in formation behind her.

"Aoléon captures the Science Academy's gia!" barked the announcer. The crowd went wild, and Gilbert jumped up and down, cheering so loudly that he almost lost his balance and fell off the hovering grandstand. Aoléon's teammates flew around her and gave her a pat on the back, congratulating her for capturing the gia.

"The Space Academy wins the game!" Blasts of psionic energy shot from the crowd into the air and exploded like a fireworks show. The Space Academy cadets were celebrating their victory.

The Science Academy floated over to Aoléon and her teammates to bow, despite the despondent looks plastered onto their faces. They bowed and flew off the field while

Aoléon and her teammates huddled together and cheered a victory cheer. The crowd joined in.

Aoléon swooped up to the Space Academy hovering grandstand and stopped right in front of Gilbert. "Whoohoo! Go, Aoléon!" shouted Gilbert over the roar of the crowd. He ran over to where Aoléon's team had gathered around her and gave her a hug, congratulating her for the win. "You were amazing! I had no idea you could fly a skyboard like that."

"Thank you," blushed Aoléon.

"Why do you think Charm would do this to you?" inquired Gilbert.

"She is insecure and was probably seeking retribution for her embarrassing performance in zero-g training today," said Aoléon shaking her head.

"Figures," said Gilbert. "So will you be able to get your board fixed?"

"Sure. I have a friend who owns a skyboard shop called SkyJammers that sponsors me. He will fix the nacelle and have it back to me in no time. Come to think of it, we can drop it off on our way home today," said Aoléon.

"How are we going to get there without your skyboard working?"

"We phase."

"Phase?"

"Yes. Superconsciousness enables certain abilities — one of which is what you Terrans would incorrectly call 'teleportation.' As fifth-level-consciousness bubbleverse beings, we can phase-matter jump to any point in third- or fourth-density-level space-time using nothing but our thoughts alone. Here, take my arm," said Aoléon.

As Gilbert grabbed her arm, he felt as if he were being sucked underwater to a great depth. He saw stars, and then everything went dark. For a moment or for an eternity, Gilbert wasn't sure, he was trapped in an infinite void. No light. No sound. No feeling. No time.

What happened next was almost too incredible to imagine. For an instant, Gilbert connected to the infinite and simultaneously manifested all points in third- and fourth-density space and time. He could sense everything, everywhere, for all time. Then it faded.

Once again, he could feel his heart pulsing rapidly in his chest. From nothing, feeling crept back into his limbs. His arms and legs tingled faintly as though they had fallen asleep. His senses slowly came back to him. He was now standing outside a building somewhere in the megalopolis far away from where he had been just an instant before. No time had passed…or had it been an eternity? Gilbert couldn't tell.

"Congratulations! You just completed your first phased-matter jump. How do you feel?"

"Zoikers! Like being squeezed through a toothpaste tube."

"Wait here, I will be just a moment," said Aoléon as she entered the shop with her skyboard and had a brief conversation with the shop owner who nodded and took the board from her. A moment later she was back on the street standing next to Gilbert.

"Mu says he will have it fixed in a day," said Aoléon. "Come on, we are going to celebrate our victory and meet my psi-ball team for evening consumption." Gilbert took her arm again, and they disappeared in a flash.

Aoléon and Gilbert arrived at Saturn Pizza — one of the favorite hangouts of the Space Academy students. On top of the building was a giant rotating holokronic projection of a Martian woman holding up a pizza platter while standing on top of the planet Saturn. Gilbert followed Aoléon inside the restaurant where they joined a dozen Martian Space Academy students chatting excitedly about the game. When they saw Aoléon, several of them stood up and cheered.

"Here she comes! The death-defying aerial acrobat herself!" said one Martian student speaking to Aoléon whose cheeks suddenly turned bright cyan.

"Come and sit here at my table," said another student.

"Hey everyone. I would like you all to meet my friend, Gilbert; he is visiting with me for a couple of days," said Aoléon, slapping him on the shoulder and motioning for him to take a seat at the table next to her.

"Hi Gilbert! Welcome to Mars!" said several students at once. Gilbert waved at them and sat down beside Aoléon at one of the hovering tables. A few moments later, a waitress floated over to their table. She wore what Gilbert thought must be gravity-displacement boots and a helmet headset to record their orders. Aoléon ordered a vegetarian galact platter, and Gilbert ordered his with asteroids on top. Both of them ordered large chocolate galactshakes with galactcream.

"So Aoléon, you took a nasty fall today. I am glad you are well," said one Martian boy. "Is your skyboard going to be all right? That engine nacelle looked in bad shape."

"I am fine, thank you. I dropped the board off at SkyJammers right before we came here, and Mu said he could have it fixed in a day."

Just then, Captain Ceti walked in with Bizwat and sat down across from Aoléon and Gilbert at their table.

"Bizwat!" cried Aoléon. "What brings you here?"

"I heard there was going to be a celebration here tonight. Someone I know took the highest fall yet still managed to win the game," said Bizwat, showing a wry grin.

"Come on Bizwat, we all played well. Ceti, Tiu, and Ptolemy played crucial roles, and Zelda created the diversion enabling us to win the game."

Ceti raised his galactshake. "Here is to the best girl to ever set foot on a skyboard. May she always have soft landings," toasted Ceti.

"Hear! Hear!" shouted Gilbert as the rest of the group raised their galactshakes and drank, leaving frothing white mustaches on their shiny blue faces.

"Say, Aoléon…on a more serious note, have you investigated what we talked about before?" queried Bizwat.

"I had planned to go tomorrow after school."

"You seem to be procrastinating…why?"

"Maybe I am. Part of me is curious, but deep down I sense that something is not right. However, the other part of me…my common sense part…tells me I am nothing but a mere Martian girl, and I should try to stay out of trouble. Who am I to intervene in something as big as this?"

"Wait one cycle…you have a common sense part?!" Bizwat chortled. "When did this happen?!" Aoléon smirked and punched him in the shoulder.

Aoléon, Gilbert, and Bizwat ended the evening in high spirits, saying their goodbyes for the night. Aoléon and Gilbert phased back to Aoléon's house. Gilbert crawled into his sleep chamber, and before he knew it, he had fallen asleep from exhaustion.

Continue the saga in
Part Three: "The Hollow Moon"

GLOSSARY

A.I. — An abbreviation for *artificial intelligence* — a thinking, sentient machine or computer.

A. I. hacking — Breaking into and manipulating artificial intelligence (see **A.I.**) to do your bidding.

AU — An abbreviation for *Astronomical Unit*. An Astronomical Unit is the mean distance between the Earth and the Sun. In 2012, the International Astronomical Union defined the distance to be 149,597,870,700 meters or about 93 million miles.

arcologies — Enormous, raised-pyramid hyperstructures that are self-contained microcities in a single, gargantuan building. They combine high population density residential habitats with self-contained commercial, food, agricultural, waste, energy, and transportation facilities.

Aurora Interceptor — A fictional interceptor version that I created for this book of the U.S. Air Force Aurora spy plane. "Aurora" was the code name for the U.S. Air Force's replacement for the SR-71 spy plane. The Aurora went into service in 1989. It was capable of flying into space without aid of rocket boosters, orbiting the Earth, and landing on the ground. It could fly at speeds in excess of Mach 12 within the atmosphere.

bovars — Martian cows that are saurian in origin, hatched from eggs, and produce a milk-like substance used in making galact (see **galact**), the main foodstuff of the Martian people.

Ciakar — A term used for *Draco Prime* — the Draconian (see **Draconian**) ruling caste. A Ciakar can range from 14 feet to 22 feet tall (4.3 meters to 7 meters tall) and can weigh up to 1,800 pounds (816 kg). The most distinguishing features of the Ciakar, the supreme leader of the Draconians, are white scales and large dragon wings — features that the other subcastes of the Draconian race do not possess. This is what distinguishes the Ciakar as royalty among the dragon race. A Ciakar also possesses some psionic power — telepathy and telekinesis; however, it is not nearly as strong as in some of the other alien races.

CQB — An abbreviation for *close quarters battle*. CQB is the art of tactical combat while indoors.

Deimos — See **Phobos and Deimos**.

Draconian — A reptiloid species originating from the constellation Orion. They were the first sentient species in our galaxy to have interstellar space travel (more than four billion years ago). Their society is based on a hierarchical caste system in which the leaders constitute a separate species known as the Ciakar (see **Ciakar**). The castes are royalty, priest, soldier, worker, and outcast.

Draco Prime — See **Ciakar.**

DUMB — An abbreviation for *Deep Underground Military Base*.

EBE — An abbreviation for *Extraterrestrial Biological Entity* — another term for alien.

ESA — An abbreviation for *European Space Agency* (NASA for Europe).

FBI — An abbreviation for *Federal Bureau of Investigation*.

galact — A milk-like substance that is the primary food for the Martian people.

GSG-9 — An abbreviation for *Grenzschutzgruppe 9*. GSG-9 is the elite counter-terrorism and special operations unit of the German Federal Police.

holokron display / holokronic display — A holographic projector and communications device.

Luminess — The spouse of the Luminon.

Luminon — The supreme ruler of Mars.

Majestic Twelve (MJ-12) — A secret committee of scientists, military leaders, and government officials formed in 1947 by an executive order of U.S. President Harry S. Truman to investigate UFO activity in the aftermath of the Roswell crash incident.

MAJIC — See **Majestic Twelve**.

MJ-12 — See **Majestic Twelve**.

nanites — Microscopic robots that perform various enhancement actions.

NASA — An abbreviation for *National Aeronautics and Space Administration*.

NOFORN — An abbreviation for *no foreign nationals*. NOFORN is a designation for classified documents that means that no foreign nationals should be permitted to see them.

NSA — An abbreviation for *National Security Agency*. The three-letter alphabet soup agency is lovingly called "no such agency" by its spook insiders. It is responsible for running the global ECHELON System — a signal intelligence-gathering network that sucks up and records all phone, satellite, Internet, and data worldwide.

NYPD — An abbreviation for *New York Police Department*.

omnitool — A hand-held computer device that can perform a multitude of functions including being able to hack door locks as well as deactivate force fields and turrets.

omniverse — The conceptual ensemble of all possible universes with all possible laws of physics.

ORCON — An abbreviation for *originator controlled*. ORCON is the intelligence marking signaling that material contained is "originator-controlled" and cannot be distributed further without the National Security Agency's permission.

paladins — See **Royal Paladin Elite Guards**.

parsec — A unit of astronomical distance in which 1 parsec = 3.26 light years or about 19 trillion miles, 1 mega-parsec =1 million parsecs or 3.262 million light years, and 1 light year = the distance light travels in one year. Long story short, it is a ludicrous distance to travel so quickly because it is a distance far beyond most people's ability to comprehend.

phase-jump — See **phase-matter jump**.

phase-matter jump — The ability to shift to the post-plasma beam state of matter and teleport yourself and others instantly to another location using only your mind.

phase-shifting — See **phasing**.

phasing — The ability to shift or change matter states. See also **phase-matter jump**.

Phobos and Deimos (moons) — The two moons of Mars that are named after the two horses of the Greek god of war meaning "fear" and "dread." They are roughly the size of large asteroids and have artificially circular orbits around the equator of Mars. The ratio of Phobos's orbital period to Deimos's orbital period is almost clock-like in that Phobos is the minute hand and Deimos the hour hand. Deimos orbits once every 30.4 hours and Phobos every 7 hours 39 minutes.

plasma — The fourth state of matter. A state of matter in which atoms and molecules are so hot that they ionize and break up into their constituent parts: negatively charged electrons and positively charged ions.

Royal Paladin Elite Guards — The select guards of the Luminon.

Schwarzschild radius — The variable radius setting that determines the size of the micro-singularity. The higher the setting, the larger the event horizon and, subsequently, the greater the area of destruction. Dialed down to its lowest setting, it could target a single individual within a crowd while leaving the others unharmed. At its maximum setting, it could destroy an entire planet. Note to operator: using this weapon at its maximum setting is inadvisable.

sentinels — Flying robotic sentries that guard Martian airspace around the megalopolis and conduct reconnaissance for the Xiocrom. Most of the time, the sentinels remain cloaked or invisible.

sentrybot — A security robot designed for basic policing and guard duty. It is less powerful than a soldierbot.

singularity — A singularity is associated with black holes. It is a situation in which matter is forced to be compressed to a point (a space-like singularity).

SITREP — An abbreviation for *situation report*.

Terra / Terrans — Terms that mean *Earth / Earthlings* and refer to the Earth and / or to people who inhabit the Earth.

umbra (classification) — The highest level of classification.

VTOL — An abbreviation for *Vertical Takeoff and Landing*. VTOL refers to an aircraft that is capable of lifting off like a helicopter and then transitioning to regular flight like an airplane.

Xiocrom — The artificial intelligence that controls all Martian governmental functions, the bot and drone workforces, and the robot invasion forces.

Note: Many of the above definitions came from Wikipedia, the free online encyclopedia. I would like to thank their many anonymous authors whose explanations have contributed to the project.

For Xena, who kept me company and made me laugh while I spent countless hours working on this book. For Dad, who helped me when times were tough, and for Mom and Aunt Gwen, who helped edit numerous drafts of this book. And for Jennifer, who inspired me to make the lead character female.

CPSIA information can be obtained at www.ICGtesting.com
Printed in the USA
LVOW05s0910290515

440421LV00004B/6/P

9 780979 128530